CINDRILL

A CINDERELLA RETELLING NOVELL

K.M. ROBINSON

To those that make the right choice...even if it takes a little while to get there.

CHAPTER 1
CINDRILL

It's entirely possible that I made the wrong choice coming here tonight. He's gorgeous in his tuxedo, smiling at the crowd, waving to his subjects. His son isn't half bad either—his smile is radiant as I look at him through my master's scope, the target falling directly on the prince's chest.

A group of people surrounds him, congratulating him on his impending nuptials. His betrothed stands next to him, now obscured by the group of well-wishers.

"Change of plans," Master murmurs. He pulls the weapon back, returning it to its hiding place. "We're going down there."

This wasn't the plan—we were supposed to kill them from the balcony and escape. My job was to be the distraction so Master wouldn't get caught. Mixing with the people was never supposed to be a part of this.

He wheels around on his heels, stalking across the walkway to the stairs. I descend first, taking my place among the partygoers. I mix with the ladies in their incredible gowns—my own matches theirs tonight.

"A dance, mistress?" A gentleman of the court holds his hand out to me—no one else is dancing.

"Oh, uh, no," I sputter. "Thank you. I haven't congratulated the prince yet. Excuse me."

"Ridiculous, petty woman," he mumbles as I flee. "She wears a green gown, and suddenly she thinks she's the Summer Queen."

I ignore him as I brush through the crowd, batting my eyelashes whenever I bump into a man. I intentionally avoid the women—they'd look too closely at me.

My new job is to clear a path for Master—I'm the distraction. He will follow behind, and while I have the attention of the crowd, he will murder the king and his son.

I tuck one of my chestnut curls behind me and breeze through the people until I'm only a few feet from the prince's bride-to-be. She's a tiny thing—she may even be younger than I am. Her hair is piled on her head in blonde ringlets that are so fair that they're nearly white. The girl is attached to the prince's arm, looking nervous.

"Vila runs a charity for orphans," Prince Davian

informs his guests. He glances at her with a forced smile —I've only been in his presence for the last hour, but even *I* can tell this arranged marriage isn't doing anything for either of them. "She's very charitable on her father's behalf."

"Won't you miss working with the children, Princess?" A woman shoves a microphone at her.

"I'm sure I'll have responsibilities here that will keep me busy, but, of course, I'll miss the children." She tries to smile, but it's clear she's upset about leaving her charity. I can't say I blame her—I'd be mad if I didn't have a choice in my life too. Or, rather, I *am* mad that I don't have a choice in my life either.

Prince Davian rattles off a list of the foreign princess' virtues. The more he talks, the higher the princess stands. Perhaps she's coming to terms with the arrangement and she's stopping the wilted flower act... or maybe she's just proud of her many accomplishments.

I'm proud of mine as well, though I can hardly imagine how the prince would spin my achievements— how *would* one describe the actions of an assistant to an assassin?

Princess Vila catches my eye and smiles, appraising my dress. While hers is full on the bottom and sleek on top, mine isn't nearly as poofy. Hers is restricted to a bell-shape at the bottom, while mine flows loose enough to run in without tripping me as I move in these ridiculous shoes.

Master's apprentice, Claude, designed the outfit for me. He has a flair for the eye-catching. The top of my dress drapes in the front and plummets in the back, revealing a good portion of my spine. My shoes are tall but solid. I couldn't roll my ankle in them if I tried—and I *had* tried just to prove a point to him. The sides of them wrap around the top of my foot in a pattern that looks like waves on the seas or arching mountains that curl over on themselves—they look as fierce and vicious as I'm supposed to be. Vila almost looks jealous of them.

"I like your shoes," she murmurs.

"Thank you, Princess. I like your gown." She smiles at me, moving her hand to smooth her already perfectly-in-place dress. Now is as good a time as any—I have to get her out of the way for Master. "Would you tell me about your charity?"

She lights up, prepared to gush. The princess tells me all about the children there and the big fundraising event she's helping them plan. It appears I'm doing the world a favor by ending her marriage before it begins—she'll go back to her orphanage and the world will be better for it.

The screams are my first indication that something is wrong. A woman sobs as the crowd shuffles. Another scream fills the air.

"Shooter!"

The prince is pulled back by a guard, leaving the princess standing alone next to me. A man nearby falls, bleeding out on the ground. The king screams as a bullet rips through his upper leg—his guards pull the king back as Master approaches.

He's clothed from head to toe in black. A hood covers his head while a cape billows out behind him just enough to look impressive, but not enough for anyone to grab onto—Claude designed it that way.

Master moves toward me, but he doesn't make eye contact. Instead, he raises his weapon toward Vila.

She wasn't part of the deal. We're not supposed to be hurting foreign dignitaries, just the king and prince. Her kingdom is a friend of Master's—they've used him on occasion to fix some of their more discrete problems. If Master kills this girl, he's bringing a war down on our heads that we likely won't survive, but he doesn't seem to care.

"No!" I shout, stepping in front of her.

My job is to protect Master, and tonight, that means I must protect him from himself, even if that means my own death.

I pull out the weapon Claude embedded in the side of my dress, hidden by the folds of my skirt. Aiming it at Master, I threaten to shoot his arm to stop him. He seethes at me as I push the princess backward.

One of the guards takes aim at Master, releasing

several bullets in our direction—one whizzes past me, nearly striking Vila around my arm stretched across her. She screams, realizing how close she came to being hit.

Master reels back, a bullet burying itself in his upper arm. As he staggers backward, I turn, forcing the princess to run. She trips over her own feet, but I drag her along, carefully pointing my weapon away from her.

The palace is a flurry of screams accompanied by pounding feet as the court runs in different directions, trying to avoid Master's assault. The hallway is my best option, and I flee with my charge in tow. She gasps behind me but manages to keep up until I push her to run in front of me, using my hands to push her faster.

"Stop!" someone screams behind me. "Unhand the princess!"

Ordinarily, they might assume I was helping her, but the majority of the palace guards saw me pull my weapon on Master and it's only logical to assume that the people with weapons are working together. In truth, we are.

More fire sounds behind me, but I don't stop. My gaze darts around the hallway, looking for an escape. I can hear Master approaching, his telltale footfall rings in my ears above all of the other noise—I've been trained far too well to miss him.

"Kill her!" Master yells to me, his voice altered by one of Claude's devices.

I round the corner and see a doorway—a closet. I fling the door open and shove the princess inside.

"Stay quiet," I hiss, shutting the door as quietly as possible before running.

The guards rush around the corner, Master suddenly quiet. He escapes somewhere in the palace and deactivates his nanobot mask to change his appearance so no one recognizes him as the shooter, leaving me to take the blame.

Before I can reach the next corner, one of the guards reaches me—I shouldn't have stopped to save the princess—and he pulls on my shoulder. Thank goodness my dress is off-the-shoulder or he would have ripped it with the way he grabs at me.

I dip down, throwing him off balance and he slips to the floor as I try to speed up.

Searing pain rips through my right foot, and I cry out. As I turn to see what happened, I lose my shoe—I've been cut. The man who attacked me must have pulled a knife as he was falling and sliced the top of my foot around the shoe's intricate design. The green heel bounces away from him.

The man on the ground looks up at me, shouting something. The knife glints in his hand, but I don't stop, even as the prince's tirade continues from his place on the marble floor.

The nanobots peel off my face, racing down my body

to my leg to form a new shoe so that I can continue to run at the same pace. I turn as quickly as possible to conceal my identity—I can't let him see my face.

The hall sounds hollow as I pound across the marble in one green heel and one silver one—or silver until the nanobots have time to change color. For now, I'll have to tolerate the mismatched colors as the nanobots do a more important job—keeping me from sliding on the slippery floor.

I dart out into the night air. The sky is black as ink, but the stars twinkle in the crisp autumn evening. Master is waiting at the end of the palace drive, and I rush down the stairs.

CHAPTER 2
DAVIAN

"A re you all right, Vila?" I hold my hand out to the princess, helping her out of the closet.

"I'd like to go to my room now, please," Vila replies. She allows me to move her into the hallway and promptly turns on her heels. Her blue dress barely swishes around her feet as she moves—I wonder if her stylists did the same thing to the skirt that they did to her hair to make it stay in place despite running.

"Of course." I bow slightly to her. "My apologies for the intrusion. You must have been terrified to have that gun held to you—I'm sure you want to rest."

She looks a little bewildered at my statement, eyes wide and brow furrowed, but she doesn't challenge me. The princess nods and her people escort her back to her room.

"You're going to do something about this, Davian." My father's suggestions always come out as commands. "Her father will not be pleased when he hears about tonight. You need to take action *now* before he finds out and cancels the wedding."

When I turn, several guards are carrying my father through the hallway. His leg is dripping blood, but it blends in with his black pants so I can only see it when it hits the floor, leaving a trail of red from the ballroom.

"Of course, Father," I reply. "We'll hunt the girl down tonight."

"You've already let her escape—just how do you plan on finding her?" he questions.

"Everyone saw her, Father. We'll send the entire Guard out to find her."

"You can't be sure it is the right girl. We can't execute her without proof," he challenges.

I swallow, looking around as I try to figure out a quick answer. Silently, I lecture myself for tripping—I could have killed the murderess on the spot if she hadn't ducked and thrown me off balance.

"Her shoe!" I exclaim, eyes landing on the strangest shoe I've ever seen. Pieces of it curl around the sides, a hideous mark stretching across the fabric between two of the curls. "I managed to cut her foot while she was fleeing and she lost the shoe. All we have to do is match her scar to the pattern on the edge of the shoe, and we'll have our proof."

My father grunts in pain as the guards nearly drop him. He glares at me as if this was *my* fault.

"Find her—tonight. If the girl is not in our custody by tomorrow evening, we might as well send that girl home ourselves." My father isn't a fan of Vila's father, but we need a merger, and a wedding is the ultimate form of an alliance. "Once you get the murderess, torture her until she tells you the name of the hooded man, and then kill them both."

With arms resting across two of the guards' shoulders to stabilize himself, he tips his head back. They carry him down the hall toward his room, bypassing the exit to the infirmary—the royal doctors will be sent for immediately, if they haven't been already.

Alone, I glance around the hallway. I quickly turn and walk toward the security office—I'm going to need all the help I can get.

The office is dark, the overhead lights off. Filip leans forward in his chair, typing notes on his tablet as he stares at the bank of glowing screens in front of him. Leaning over, he says something into one of the microphones, releasing his hold on the button once he finishes speaking.

"Figured you'd show," he mumbles, knowing I had arrived before I announced myself.

"What happened?" I ask, taking a seat next to him. I cross my arms over each other and lean forward onto my knees, jaw tight.

"Looks like there was a team. They were pretty amazing about avoiding the cameras," he responds, still flipping switches and hitting buttons as he assesses the playback of the attack. "You can't even see them until they're right next to you. It looks like the girl came from the stairs, but I have no idea where the hooded man came from."

"She threw Vila in a closet."

Filip pauses to turn to me.

"She what?" He shakes his head. "No, never mind. As long as she's not dead, I don't care."

"It doesn't make sense that an assassin would choose *not* to murder someone, does it?"

"Maybe her orders were only to kill you and your father." He shrugs, turning away from me to work.

"She went out of her way to save Vila, Filip. And the other guy specifically told her to kill the princess." None of this makes any sense.

"I don't understand how these cameras went out. Look, " he mumbles, changing the conversation as he points at one of the monitors. "All of these cameras went out at the same time—they must have taken them down somehow or else I'd have footage of everything. I saw you talking to your father in the hallway after, but nothing before that—aside from you chivalrously pulling Vila out of the closet."

He shoots me a look to indicate my *chivalry* had been a little lacking. It's not my fault—I've tried to talk to the princess before, it's just not working well.

"So, you don't have *anything* for me?" I sigh.

"Not unless you can give me any information."

I quickly recount the scene in the ballroom, giving him as much detail as possible. He takes notes on everything, inputting it into his tablet so he can give assignments to his men when we're done.

"I've never seen anything like it, Filip." I run my hands through my hair. "Her face just…peeled off."

"Peeled off?" He looks at me as though I've lost my mind. Maybe I have.

"It was like her entire face shattered. I don't know how to explain it."

The girl's deep brown hair bounced with each step she took as she ran down the hall—she looked like she was straight out of a movie the way she moved. The green of her dress offset her pale skin, and if I hadn't wanted to kill her, I might have wanted to pursue her for other reasons. Not that I can do that anymore—I'm getting married.

Filip's face twitches like he wants to say something. Eventually, he turns back.

"I don't know how to explain that, but I think the

most important thing right now is to figure out where she went." He nods, reaching for his control panel. One of the monitors switches as I stare at an image of the outside of the palace. "They escaped—we know that much for sure."

"Father wants me to find her before tomorrow."

His eyebrows shoot up as he turns to me again.

"Before tomorrow?" His face grows cold. "Why?"

"Vila's father will pull out of the deal once he finds out his daughter was almost shot," I explain. "If we can't show him we handled the situation swiftly, we could have a serious problem on our hands."

"What do you need me to do?" Filip asks. He waits patiently as I explain about the shoe and how we'll conduct a search for the girl with the matching injury at first light.

"Okay, I'm in. We can leave Sturges in charge for a few days while I'm helping you hunt down the huntress."

"Huntress?"

"Murderess?" He shrugs, getting up to lead the way down the hall to find his second-in-command. "I don't know, pick a name, but I'm not traipsing around this kingdom with you without having something interesting to call her."

He pauses, straightening his shoulders.

"If you make *one* shoe joke while we're out there…" he pretends to threaten me. He knows me too well.

"Fine, no shoe jokes. You had to go and shoo away all my fun before we could even get started, didn't you?"

He grumbles beside me.

One way or another, we'll find that girl, and when we do, we'll get everything we need from her.

CHAPTER 3
CINDRILL

The air is damp with early morning dew as I pull my hood over my head. My curls peek out annoyingly, and I attempt to tuck them back in the fabric.

I slink around the building, tugging on the pack Master sent with me until it sits more comfortably on my back. The weight over the small of my back is comforting.

A bird chirps somewhere in the distance, but the sound is crisp. I accidentally step in a patch of grass and have to pause to shake my boot off—I don't want to be covered in dew.

The sun is barely slipping over the horizon, and I shiver as the breeze brushes across my cheek. Master's friend won't wait long for me, so I don't have time to dawdle. I round the corner…and slam into the wall.

Pushing, I fight my attacker off behind me. He doubles over when I stomp on his foot. Yelling erupts as I throw my elbow into his nose, breaking it with a loud crack.

"Enough! Stop her!" a familiar voice shouts as several sets of hands grab hold of me. Struggling against them does nothing to help me. I jolt to a stop, torso moving forward while the men hold my shoulders in place painfully.

I look up into the eyes of the Prince Davian. He stares back at me, scrutinizing me with narrowed, hazel eyes as he tries to place me. I glare at him from under my long, swooping bangs.

He can't recognize me—he didn't see me without the nanobot mask last night. If I keep my mouth shut, I might be able to escape.

"What are you doing out here?" His voice is lower than it was last night. It's dark and gravely—just as I'd expect this early in the morning.

"Running errands, Your Majesty," I reply quietly, bowing my head.

"What errands?" His nose wrinkles as he speaks, lip curling up slightly.

"I'm picking up some parts for my father," I lie.

"For?" The prince sounds aggravated. His hands clench at his sides.

"He's a clockmaker, Your Majesty," I repeat the lines I've rehearsed with Master so many times before.

"And have you retrieved these items yet?" The prince frowns at me, not believing my story.

"Yes, sire." I turn to adjust the bag on my back where I've stored enough clock pieces to back my lie up. Opening my hand, I reveal several cogs.

"Very well," he replies tersely. "Check her."

The men lunge at me again, digging their hands into my arms. I cry out in pain—not because I can't tolerate it, but because it's part of my escape plan.

One of the men yanks the hem of my skirt away from my feet, and I scream in surprise, kicking at him. My foot slams into his face, cracking his nose. He reels back and bares his teeth at me.

"Unhand me," I protest angrily. *No one* gets to mess with my wardrobe and live.

Knowing I can't escape—*nor should I try*—I restrict myself to throwing one elbow back, crashing into a second guard who stumbles behind me.

"Touch me again and I'll break all of your noses," I threaten. Turning to the prince, I stare him down, challenging him. His eyebrow ticks up slightly, and he smirks as if he's amused at my antics.

"I suggest you cooperate miss, or else this won't end

pleasantly for you."

"Why—you'll kill me?" I snap. I shouldn't try to take on Prince Davian, but my tongue can't help itself.

"Hmm, perhaps prison *would* do you some good."

"Doubtful," I mutter. If he tries to lock me up, I'll poison the guards and escape—it wouldn't be hard. The nanobots would form a pick, and I'd be out before he had any idea what was going on.

"Excuse me?" he yelps, surprised at how outspoken I am.

"May I go home now?"

"No. We have to check your foot first."

I blink at him.

I shouldn't do it...but I do it anyway.

"Why, do you have some sort of foot fetish, Your Highness?" I bite back my smile as he gapes at me, shocked at my words. "Relax, I won't tell anyone."

"No...I...no," he stumbles. Davian throws his shoulders back and turns to his guards. "Check her."

One of the men strings his arms through mine, pinning them behind me as he pulls me against his chest. I slam my foot into his, forcing him to release me when he instinctually curls over to protect himself. I lift my skirt and hold the wrong foot out to the prince.

"They will not touch me," I inform him before eyeing the shoe one of the men is holding—*my* shoe. "If you're so bold as to demand to see my foot, *you* will do the honors."

"He will do no such thing—" one of the men growls. I pull my hand back to hit the one approaching me.

"All right!" Davian shouts, stepping forward. "But you know if you even *look* like you're going to try to hurt me, you'll be put to death."

"I wouldn't *dare* hurt the prince of Davengreen," I say innocently. I add in my sweetest voice, "And you'll be sparing your men whatever fate will befall them if they come near me again."

He takes the shoe from his guard and hesitantly steps toward me. Slowly, he lowers himself to the ground and holds the shoe out to me. I'm still balanced on my right foot, and he coughs, nodding for me to switch feet. I drop my left one and slip out of my right knee-high boot.

The nanobots blend in perfectly with my skin, covering what will likely end up as a nasty scar from the prince's knife. Davian slips the shoe on my foot, glancing up at me.

"Perfect fit," he muses. I glance away, pretending to be disinterested as he slides the shoe off my foot—I wish I could take it back to Claude. "How are you standing so perfectly still?"

"Good balance, Your Highness." I step back into the shoe I had been wearing and straighten my shoulders.

"You must be wondering what this is about," he comments, gauging my reaction.

"When the Prince of Davengreen tells me to do something, I comply without question, Your Majesty."

"Correct me if I'm wrong, but didn't you just question me?"

"I questioned your men," I indulge in correcting the prince, tipping my head quietly to one side—men have always found it hypnotizing when I shift my hair and the prince is no different.

I spot movement from the corner of my eye. A man and a younger girl attempt to back around the corner out of sight, but the guards take notice. When they attempt to drag the young girl out from behind the building, the man darts forward, brandishing a weapon.

He lunges at the prince, but I can't let the royal die yet —Master will be furious if I let these people destroy his plans. If the prince dies before the king, our plan will fail.

My body starts moving before I command it to, attempting to block the prince from the man's knife. He grabs hold of Davian, wrapping an arm around his throat, knife to the side of his neck.

"Let her go!" the man demands.

The prince's eyes are wide, but he stays calm, assessing his situation with nearly the same precision Master trained me to use. I allow tears to well up in my eyes as if I'm frightened and openly turn into a sniveling mess, leading the man to believe I'm no threat.

"Please don't hurt him," I beg through my fake tears.

The man looks at me, face twitching.

"Let my daughter go," he growls, nearly sounding like it's a question rather than a statement.

I could potentially take his daughter captive and force a trade, but I need to get the prince out of his grip, and I doubt the guards will let me get near the girl.

Slipping out of my shoe as I step forward, I use my wrap-around skirt to cover my movements—I'm grateful I chose to wear it along with my faux-leather pants. I take an uneven step toward them.

"They're just trying shoes on people," I inform the man. "They did it to me, and I'm fine."

The daughter is sobbing in the confinement of the guards' arms. She struggles against them, hands wrapped around their beefy arms.

"Why are you trying the shoes on us?" I ask the prince as if I don't already know. When he doesn't answer, I repeat myself, sounding suspicious of him.

"It belongs to a murderess," he finally growls at me. "If it fits, we've found the killer."

"It could fit hundreds of girls!" the man shouts, tightening his grip on the prince's neck.

"No!" At his outburst, the man lets go just enough so that Davian can breathe again. He coughs. "The pattern has to match. There's only one girl it could fit."

"So if your daughter didn't murder anyone, it won't fit her and they'll let us all go." I try to sound as desperate as possible as I turn to the man holding the prince at knifepoint.

The man swings around to look at me, giving me a mere second to lash out at him. I grab the knife from my belt that I carefully hid from the royal guards and jam it into the man's upper arm. He shrieks in pain. When he recoils, he accidentally sets the prince free.

Reaching out, I flip the man over, wrestling him to the ground until he is subdued. Two guards tackle him as the daughter screams. I rush to her side to make her comply before the guards do.

"I will not be sent to prison because *you* made a stupid choice," I threaten her. Propelling her back against the wall of a building, I grab the shoe and force her to try it on. Her feet are much larger than mine, and when it's clear it can't be her, I knock her out, slamming the hilt of my knife into her temple.

Whipping around, I move quickly over to the father and leave him in an unconscious pile on the cobblestone walk as well.

"I have done as you asked, *and* I have protected you, Your Majesty. I would like to go home now." Making demands of the prince isn't wise, but it's my only chance to have the upper hand.

He grins at me, taking a long step toward me around the man's unconscious body.

That was a mistake.

CHAPTER 4
DAVIAN

"No, you'll be coming with us, madam." I know better than to let someone with her talents go. I've never seen anyone diffuse a situation so quickly—not even the elite guards my father has following us around whenever we leave the palace.

"I must return home," she insists, clutching her bag strap in her hand. She shifts uncomfortably, looking nervous.

"You don't have anything to hide, do you?" I try to sound carefree, but I know better. Even if this girl isn't the murderess I'm hunting, someone has trained her to protect herself—nothing about this girl is ordinary.

She reaches up, tucking a strand of curly, brown hair behind her ear. Her finger snags on her hood, tugging it off-center adorably.

Wait, no. Not *adorably. She is not adorable; she is dangerous.*

"I have nothing to hide."

"Good, then you can assist me on my mission. Obviously you're skilled enough to help me. Once we find the woman we're looking for, you may go. Until then, you'll join my personal team of guards in the search for the assassin that tried to murder my father last night. Having a female with us will make the women we're testing more comfortable."

Her eyes grow wide, revealing green the color of grass. I take a moment to examine her, noting her tight-fitting, long-sleeved, hooded shirt and sleek black pants surrounded by a partial skirt—just enough to look feminine while also looking deadly. I wonder what her story is.

"Come," I motion to the side. She steps out into the lead, following my orders even though she doesn't know where we're going. I eye Filip, and he nods briefly, assuring me that he'll watch the girl. "What is your name?"

I catch up to her with Filip right behind us, weapon carefully hidden just out of her sight. She glances over at me, a strand of her curls toppling out of her hood on the opposite side.

"Does it matter, Majesty?" She speaks so curtly to me that I can't help but chuckle.

"I am Davian," I introduce myself.

"I'm aware."

When this is all over, I'm going to put a tracker on her just to see what she does with herself—she's so intriguing. She doesn't seem at all worried that I could have her arrested or even killed if she angers me in any way—not that I would ever kill someone over that.

"This is the part where you tell me *your* name," I whisper playfully, hoping to get her to let her guard down.

"Oh, but isn't it more fun to keep it a secret and play the game?" she counters flirtatiously. The girl tucks her curls back again, letting her fingers linger near her chin —she's good.

"You can either tell me your name, madam, or I can assign you one, but I'm not going to guess." I don't mind playing games, but it will be on *my* terms.

She considers my words before finally relenting, shoulders sagging. Taking a deep breath, she softly speaks.

"Cindrill."

That's the strangest name I've ever heard, and I wonder if she's made it up. It doesn't matter—I have a name to call her, and once we're all done, I'll bring her back to the palace to interrogate her.

"Very well then, Cindrill," I address her as formally as I can. "We're looking for a murderess who visited the palace last night. She was wearing a green dress and those shoes we made you try on. She and her partner were trying to murder my father, fiancée, and me."

She cringes as I explain, but reaches up to knock her hood off, fully revealing her hair. It cascades halfway down her back in loose curls—the photographers would have a field day with her if she ever visited the palace. If she didn't make me so nervous, I might actually invite her to the palace for an event other than an interrogation simply to add to the aesthetic of a gathering.

"If you were bent on destroying someone and your plan was ruined, where would you hide out?" The question is casual enough. I shrug a shoulder and glance over at her. I can feel Filip judging her response behind me.

"I wouldn't," she responds lightly. "You'd be expecting that. I'd stay close to the palace and remain in plain sight. *Did you* check near the palace?"

The guards checked last night, but admittedly, not this morning.

"I'll take that as a no," she adds. "So you and your men just ran out this morning before the sun could come up to…*what*—run around and corner girls going to the market?"

"Well, we couldn't very well order all the women in the country to the palace doorstep for this, now could we?" I huff. I don't like that she is challenging my decision. "Besides, this way, we won't miss anyone."

"You and your team of *twenty men* won't miss anyone? You'd be better off shooting a couple of arrows from atop the palace walls and hoping it hits the assassin." Filip snorts behind me. "I don't think you've thought this through very well."

"Then just what would you suggest we do, *Miss Cindrill?*"

"Drop the *miss*," she corrects me. "I would set a trap, of course. Why go traipsing around the countryside when you could draw the assassin to you? If you plan it right, you can pull her in, catch her, and not have a hair on your precious royal head harmed in the process."

"And if it's not planned right, he dies. Brilliant," Filip scoffs.

"What kind of a trap?" I ignore my head of security.

"*Another ball*, perhaps?"

"That wasn't a ball," I mutter.

"Close enough." She sounds exasperated. "I've seen your court go in and out of there with their fancy gowns and suits—you can't convince me you're not throwing lavish events inside of those walls."

"It was an engagement party—not everything we do inside that palace is fun, Cindrill."

"Remind me of that during the royal wedding," she sneers at me. I don't think she's thrilled with the idea of me marrying the princess of Briarmar.

"Are you angling for an invitation?" I ask, catching her

off guard. Her gaze shoots over to me, eyes wide again. It's fun throwing her off-kilter a bit.

"Oh, I wouldn't be caught dead in the palace," she replies, her smile dark. "Your guards wouldn't know what to do with me even if I *did* show up."

"I have a feeling you're right there."

"We're almost there, sire," Filip says from behind us. Glancing up, I see the town square looming in front of us, the tall processing building standing high above the rest as it towers over the town.

"We're going to the Epicenter?"

"How else do you expect us to corral all these women?"

"Bat your eyelashes, of course," she mutters under her breath. I whip around to look at her, my own eyes wide this time, and snort, unable to keep my laughter in.

"Is that really what you think of me?"

"That's what *everyone* thinks of you, Prince Davian." It's the first time she's said my name, and she makes it sound even more regal than the court announcer does. "The world bows at the feet of the prince with the pretty face—your fiancée must be thrilled."

My fiancée and I don't even know each other—I doubt she's thrilled that other women think I'm nice to look at.

"You like my face, huh?" I'm not flirting with her—not really. I'm arranged to marry Vila and everyone knows it, and this girl clearly doesn't like me anyway, so there's no harm in having the same type of conversation I've always had with people.

"What's your plan once we reach the Epicenter?"

"Well, I thought perhaps *you* would be able to help me spot anyone who looks like they're worried."

"This is never going to work," she grumbles, adjusting the bag on her shoulder. I probably should have had Filip check her bag more thoroughly, but if she hasn't used anything against us yet, we're probably safe.

We walk through the large doors to the Epicenter. Each town in the kingdom has one, and every morning, the majority of people pass through it to check in for work. They're shuttled to different locations once they've signed in, and at the end of the day, they're returned home. Only people that work within the center of town don't have to make an appearance at the Epicenter to travel to work.

The building is grand, with tall columns built into the walls that stretch high above our heads. The Epicenter is several stories tall, the second and third levels a mix of offices and bay doors for workers to step on and off the shuttles.

"Your majesty," the man at the entrance says, looking shocked. He gapes, unsure of whether to request I place my hand on the bio scanner or not. I step up to it and do it without his prompting.

"Thank you," I say, stepping forward. Cindrill gasps behind me as one of the men pushes her to the scanner, directing her.

When I turn, she's hesitantly placing her hand on the glass covering the device. The light shines around her, reading her biometrics. It dings when the scan is complete.

"I'm here against my will," she proclaims to the man who looks uncomfortable. When he does nothing, she huffs and steps forward.

"The prince kidnapped me, oh no," I mock her. "Did you really think that would work?"

"I think I'm establishing a trail. If anything should happen to me, my father will come looking, and if people know you took me, he'll know to stop searching for me so nothing bad happens to him too." Her honesty is refreshing—no one speaks to me like this.

"I'm not going to harm you, Cindrill, I just need your help."

"To execute a girl," she points out, using her finger to emphasize her point. "You want me to help find a girl that you're going to kill."

"She tried to kill *me*."

"That makes it so much better." She shakes her head but suddenly perks up. "There."

I turn to see where she's pointing at. A woman in her early thirties clicks across the lobby paying us no mind.

She's too old to be the woman I saw last night, but it's a good test for Cindrill.

"Let's go see if it's her." I let her take the lead. Filip follows behind us, carrying the marked-up shoe.

"Ma'am," Cindrill calls out. "Please stop. The prince needs a word with you."

The woman freezes when she hears my title, slowly turning back to face us. She drops into an immediate curtsey, nearly dropping the tablet in her hand.

Cindrill quickly explains that she must try the shoe on, but gives her no explanation as to why. She drops the shoe on the ground in front of the woman and allows her to steady herself on her arm covered in dark brown fabric.

"No match," Cindrill announces. She waits as the woman takes off the shoe and slips back into her own before dropping her arm. She looks from Filip to the shoe, refusing to pick it up—one of the other guards gets it.

The room begins to bustle and my men direct all of the women who fit the correct age range into a line as they wait to try on the shoe. The process takes forever, but Cindrill holds remarkably still the entire time. I, on the other hand, can't stand still.

When the line finally dies down, one of my men approaches us, tension lines stretched across his face.

Filip catches sight of him and demands to know what it is.

"That woman skipped the line," the guard huffs as if he's been running—he hasn't. "She claimed she had to get to work and didn't have time for this. I couldn't stop her."

My heart starts racing—she has to be the one.

"Go!" I demand, forcing my men into action. They all race away to apprehend the woman, leaving me to finish testing the last eight women with Cindrill.

"Last call!" a man yells, and the women in front of me panic as they realize they will miss the final shuttle to their workplaces.

"Come along." I wave them forward. Stumbling, I force them to try on the shoe as we hurry toward the platform to catch the shuttle. Cindrill tries to keep them from tripping, but it's no use.

"Prince Davian," she lectures as a redhead nearly crashes to the floor while still holding onto Cindrill.

I stoop down to hold the shoe out to the next woman, mere inches from the shuttle bay, but the door starts to slide shut, and the rest of the people push inside. They take me with them, separating me from my guards.

CHAPTER 5
CINDRILL

The prince stumbles backward, catching his foot on the edge of the shuttle. He falls to the ground, looking up in horror as the doors start to whoosh shut—the shuttle stops for no one.

The guards are too far away to help, leaving the prince on his own. I throw myself between the doors, slamming into a rider just as the door misses my foot. I glance down at the prince, unsure of what to do.

This is a brilliant opportunity for me—I could take him to Master, and we could hold the prince for ransom to get the king in front of Master's scope, too, or I could hide him away and try to get information from him. I have the rest of the shuttle ride to figure it out, but one thing I know is that Prince Davian will not be returning home tonight.

"Is that the prince?" someone murmurs.

"Where are his guards?" an older woman sounds worried for his safety.

"His guards aren't here?" This man's voice is far more eager. He must be a part of one of the resistance groups that wants to remove the crown and force an insane group of rebels with plans of grandeur onto the thrown to control the people for their own personal gain.

The blond man looks around, his curly hair tossing as he searches for Davian.

"We have to go," I whisper harshly, holding my hand down to Davian. He swallows but takes my hand, assuming he's safer with me than with the rebel—and he is...for now.

He staggers to his feet, and I push him in front of me as I force him down the tiny aisle, crashing into people. We make it to the next car, slipping through the crowd.

"We have to get you out of sight," I hiss. "We're getting off at the next stop."

"What if *he* gets off?"

"We stay on," I reply, annoyed that he doesn't know this already.

I push him into the front corner of the car, hoping to be overlooked if the curly haired man comes through the doors. I'm not as tall as the prince, but I attempt to use my body to block him.

We wait quietly, heads tipped down low together. His

breathing is heavy, even though we didn't run. In my nervousness, I adopt his breathing pace and match him without meaning to.

The door clicks open, the tell-tale swoosh announcing that we have been followed. Davian is looking at me when I glance up.

"He's here," he mouths.

"Trust me?" I ask quickly before pressing my body against his. I wrap my arm around his neck and turn his face into me to use my hair to conceal his features.

Davian wraps his arms around me, getting the picture. His fingers graze over the small of my back and down my hips. I shiver.

He grins against my cheek and uses his hands to run up my back as if it's a game. His nose is against mine, the tip brushing just under my eye as he gets closer to me. An arm wraps around my waist again, dragging me closer to him.

Fine, two can play at this game.

I reach up, entangling my fingers in his hair and I feel his lips part against my cheek in surprise. Sighing, I drag my left hand down his shoulder to his chest making him shudder into me. A little breath of air escapes his lips as I decide to torture him more.

Pushing up on my toes, I pull his face against my neck and raise my shoulder to cradle his head. I yank hard on his hip, shifting his entire body to the side as I pull him away from the wall he's resting against.

He gives in slowly, cautiously putting his lips against my neck as he holds back a groan—I have him right where I want him. Pulling back, I look over my shoulder for the man with the curly hair, but I think he's moved on in search of Davian elsewhere. When I turn back, the prince is blinking rapidly.

"He's gone." I drop my hands from him, pulling away. Turning my back, I stride away, waiting for him to follow me. I leave the car, traveling back to the original part of the shuttle we had entered.

After a moment, the prince joins me.

"That was—"

"You're safe," I interrupt him. "At least for now, but we really need to get you out of this shuttle. I don't care if he gets off at the next stop, we're leaving."

The prince doesn't say anything. He hovers just over my shoulder until the shuttle lurches to a stop.

"Come on," I direct, stepping toward the door.

I glance around but can't tell if the man stepped off of the shuttle or not. It doesn't matter—I have to get Davian out of the public eye if this is going to work.

"Where are we going?" Davian asks, trudging after me. I thought he might have trouble keeping up, but he seems to do just fine.

"Anywhere that's out of sight."

"Is that the *prince*?" a woman asks loudly.

"I don't suppose we should stop to try the shoe on them?" Davian asks. I think he's joking, but I can't quite tell.

"Give me that thing." I have no idea where the shoe was while we were pretending to kiss, but if I can get it back in my bag, I can probably return it to Claude without getting into too much trouble.

He doesn't question me and hands it over. Slipping it into my bag, I feel whole again—but then, when do shoes *not* make me feel that way?

"Do you know where we're going?" Davian searches for answers. I can't say I blame him—I'd want to know too.

"I've been here a few times before," I lie—I've been here *many* times. "I think there's a place we can hide over this way.

I steer us away from the crowded part of town, hoping to keep him out of an area where he could get word to his guards. We duck into an alleyway, curving around a dumpster filled with things I don't want to know about. Davian makes a face but doesn't say anything—perhaps it's time for an economics lesson.

I guide us around the town, aiming directly for the poorer outskirts where I can put on a good show for the spoiled prince. He draws closer to me the deeper we walk into the sketchier area.

"Oh dear, I guess I didn't really know where I was going," I announce, secretly grinning to myself.

"Stay close," the prince says, not sounding afraid at all. I look at him in surprise, and he protectively steps closer to me. "Just stay by me and we'll be okay."

A group of men step out from their homes, stalking toward us—they don't like visitors. We're far enough away that we can make a clean escape, but I figure a bit of a run would do Davian's royal legs some good—I hear they're insured anyway.

I tug on him and we start running as the men chase after us—they weren't close enough to get a good look at the prince's face so they give up after a few blocks. Had they realized my companion could have been the ticket to their next payday, I imagine the scene would have played out differently.

A woman lunges out of nowhere, grabbing onto my arm. She twists me around to face her, jerking me to a stop.

"Please!" she begs. "Please help us."

The woman becomes incoherent, pulling on my arm and babbling nonsense. I'm assuming she took something. Reaching up through her arm, I bring mine down so that I release her locked joint and fold her arm in two at the elbow. She sobs as I push her away, but a man walks up behind us and attempts to throw his arms around me.

Davian leaps forward, beating the man until he quickly releases me. The prince pulls me toward him and we take off down the street, leaving the two to come out of whatever intoxicated state they're in.

"Are you okay?" Davian asks, spinning me toward him.

"Fine. You?" I'm more concerned about the royal in front of me than I am for myself. The man managed to slice my arm open with his knife, but the nanobots crawled up my leg from inside my tall boot where they had been covering my cut skin and already started working on the injury on my arm—they scurry away under my sleeve when the prince notices the blood.

"You're bleeding," he gasps.

"I'm fine. We should go."

"We need to take care of your arm." He gives me a stern look as if he's not taking no for an answer.

The prince wrenches my arm toward him so he can examine the injury. He reaches inside his tailored waist-coat and pulls out a small package. When he unravels it, I discover he's been carrying around some strange form of a first aid kit.

"You don't honestly think they'd let me out of the palace without medical supplies on my person, do you?" He looks at me incredulously. "You're interesting, Cindrill, but a little naïve."

There are fourteen different ways I could kill him with that kit right now. *If only he knew.*

He quietly bandages my cut while I keep an eye out for anyone that might happen upon us. I can feel the nanobots skittering up my arm and over my shoulder toward the small of my back where they will rest until they can return to the injury to repair it.

"Good as new," the prince murmurs. "Now we just need to get back to the palace district."

"Of course, Your Majesty."

"Are you really okay, Cindrill?" He looks as if he's actually concerned for me. I still don't buy it.

"I'm fine, Your Majesty."

"At this point, I don't think calling me by my title is going to do us any good."

"What do you expect me to call you?"

"Davian," he replies. "That *is* my name."

"I doubt the general public will think that I have any right to call you by your name."

"Just try it and see how it goes," he baits me.

I frown. He grins back at me. Squinting my eyes at him does no good—he only squints back in an attempt to make me laugh.

"We're wasting time."

"Time spent with a pretty girl is never a waste of time," he throws back at me. His face suddenly falls as he realizes his mistake. "I guess I can't talk like that anymore, now can I? Sometimes I forget I'm betrothed. Can we pretend I didn't say that?"

At least he thinks I'm pretty—I can use that to my advantage—especially after the shuttle ride.

"I can't image Princess Vila would be happy about that, so yes, we can forget it." I start to walk away but pause to peer back over my shoulder. "Just name your first child after me and we'll call it even."

His jaw drops and I laugh. Waving him forward, relief washes over his face.

"So, tell me about this princess of yours," I comment. I figured I should get him to talk about himself so he doesn't ask questions about *me*.

"Uhh, well...she's my fiancée," he comments, sounding more like a question than a statement.

"Yes, I heard that." I smirk. Clearly the prince knows nothing about his bride-to-be. "What is she like? Is she pretty?"

"Yes."

"That's it? *Yes*?" I refuse to let this go.

"She's beautiful, of course—"

"What color eyes does she have?" I cut him off.

"Blue...I think. Yes, blue." He huffs in aggravation. "You're not going to let this go, are you? I barely know the girl, and you know that. She's only been here for a month."

"An entire month and you don't know the girl's eye color? True love, right here, folks. True love."

"We're still getting to know each other," he protests, sulking. I'm sure my words sting.

"You're going to marry this princess and yet you know nothing about her after a *month*? Really, Davian, she's a person, not a possession."

"Of course she's not," he snips before relenting. "She's a treaty."

"Oh, so much better."

"Fine then, if you're so smart, tell me about *your* boyfriend. Is he going to beat me up when he finds out I ran off with you today?"

"No boyfriend, so I think you're safe." Safe from a *jealous* man, anyway. Master is anything *but* jealous, and he's out for blood.

"*You're* single?" He runs his hand through his hair—which is even prettier up close—and gives me a look indicating that he doesn't believe me.

"I have better things to do than chase after boys all day."

Actually, to be fair, that's *exactly* what I do all day—they just don't survive long after I find them, thanks to Master.

"I'm sure they chase after *you* though..." he leads, bumping me with his elbow.

"Yes," I reply in a deadpan voice. "And I do to them

what I did to that girl and her father back in the palace district."

His step falters, and I imagine he's turning white, but I don't stop to look.

"You don't seriously knock people out, do you?" He rushes to catch up with me.

"Yes."

"Did your father teach you that?" he challenges.

From the corner of my eye, I see a movement in the shadows of the alleyway we're walking down—Master has arrived. He must have realized something was wrong when I didn't return to base, and he came out looking for me. I'm sure he found footage of me somewhere wandering off with the prince and now he's come to collect his prize.

An arrow whizzes past us, landing with a thunk in the door of a building. The prince pulls back, trying to locate the source of the arrow, but I whip the door open and pull the prince inside, slamming it shut behind us.

"Run," I command and point him toward the stairs.

Master will follow closely, but he's not ready to wound the prince yet—he's just pushing us toward where he wants us to go.

I follow the prince up the stairs, slamming my feet into each wooden step to go faster. We burst through another doorway and find ourselves in a bedroom that looks like it hasn't been used in the last year. A layer of dust covers everything, there are no sheets on the mattress, and there's no technology to be found anywhere.

"The window," I shout.

Davian flings the frame open, and I quickly crawl out onto a nearly flat rooftop.

"You've got to be kidding me," the prince exclaims.

"Would you prefer meeting the person with the arrows?" I call over my shoulder as I rush along the rooftop—there's no harm in making the prince work for his temporary freedom.

He doesn't see it yet, but the only way off of this roof is to jump.

CHAPTER 6
DAVIAN

My guide's half skirt billows out behind her as she races along the roof like a cat. I tried that once when I was a child, and my mother scolded me so badly that I never tried it again.

I feel off balance up on top of the building. The shingles are tipped slightly—I assume so rain can run off of it —but it makes every step I take uneven. I feel as though I'm pulled to the right every time I move.

"Hurry up," she hisses at me, still racing across the roof.

Suddenly, she picks up speed.

An arrow flies between us, stopping me in my tracks.

"Davian!" she shouts, spinning to see where I am.

"Arrow!" I call back, and her face drops.

"We have to jump!" she calls, turning to run.

"What?" There's no way I'm jumping off a building.

Everything speeds by me in a blur as I match her pace. I can see the tops of trees in my peripheral vision, and the reds, browns, and grays of other roofs, but nothing is clear.

Cindrill launches herself into the air, gliding from one roof to the next—I don't know how she didn't get caught on the ledge.

"You can make it!" she screams, waiting for me.

Another arrow slams into the roof just behind my feet.

I jump.

Wind rushes around hair, forcing it back behind me. It tears at my clothing momentarily and I'm glad I wore the gear that I did to go out in public.

The ledge fills my vision as I sail toward it—I'm not going to make it. Cindrill's face tells me as much when she charts the course of my trajectory. She races forward, leaning out over the edge.

Stretching my hands up, I slam into the side of the building. One hand catches the ledge painfully, and Cindrill's nails dig into my wrist. I attempt to climb up, using my feet to push myself up the side of the building.

Between that and Cindrill's clawing at me, I manage to make it over the ledge. We collapse behind the short wall of the ledge, trying to catch our breath while still evading the person shooting at us.

"Do you think he knows who I am?"

"Possibly." She sounds out of breath. I pull her to my chest to calm her down and comfort her—she did, after all, just save my life. I suppose I'll have to reward her later —perhaps with an invitation to the royal wedding.

My heart is beating faster than it ever has before and catching my breath is a task in and of itself, but her presence calms me…until another arrow hits.

"Time to go," she says, quickly pushing up off my chest.

She darts across the open rooftop, and I have to hope for the best as I race behind her. Without thinking, I follow her over the edge of the building, and we cascade downward.

I jolt to a stop when we hit a pile of hay.

"How did you know that would be there?" I gasp.

"Lucky guess," she admits. Tugging my hand, she pulls me down the street and around the corner.

"We've got to find somewhere to hide, Cindrill."

"Really, do you think? I thought we could head to the park and take a leisurely stroll instead."

"I'll thank you kindly to take this seriously, madam." I puff as we run.

"Oh, we're back to *madam*, are we?"

The way her lips quirk up when she's sarcastic is enchanting. I consider grabbing her hand to force her to listen to me, but I know that would be a mistake.

"Have you ever considered working for my father?" I ask instead.

"Excuse me?" She risks a glance at me before peeling around another corner.

"My father could use someone like you—I imagine you'd be quite good at spy work."

"I have no interest in being a spy," she says like it leaves a bad taste in her mouth.

Cindrill gasps when she nearly runs face first into my guards.

"Your Highness!" they shout when they see me. The men raise their weapons to Cindrill.

"Stand down," I bark at them. "She's been helping me."

"We saw her get on the shuttle with you."

"Yes, to make sure that I wasn't alone—it's a good thing too, there was a rebel who recognized me, and she prevented him from finding me." I spare them the details.

Filip pulls me to the side while the others surround Cindrill.

"What happened?" His eyes bore holes through me. "Did she try anything?"

"No, she stayed with me on the shuttle and then tried to get us back to the palace district."

"You didn't think to reach out to us?"

In truth, I hadn't. I was too busy running for my life and trying to figure Cindrill out.

"We were shot at," I inform him without emotion. "We ended up jumping off a roof to escape the guy."

"Do you think it was the assassin?"

"I don't know." I shake my head. "This guy used arrows, not bullets."

"And you don't think someone could change weapons?"

"I don't know, Filip," I say pointedly. "I think that's what we pay *you* for."

He narrows his eyes but doesn't say anything—he always does that when he's mad at me but can't say anything.

"We need to go back to the palace—your father is furious."

"I'm sure." I glance around and find Cindrill staring at me. I wonder how upset *her* father is right now. I'm sure an invitation to the palace would smooth things over— unless he doesn't like the crown, which *would* explain Cindrill's hostility toward me. Perhaps I should rethink this.

"She looks pretty uncomfortable." Filip muses without actually turning to look at the girl.

"I don't think she likes you." I smirk back.

"She doesn't look as put together as she did before, either..." He narrows his eyes in a friendly manner. "Something I should know about, Your Highness?"

On occasion, Filip lets his professionalism-guard

down and treats me like a friend—but only on rare occasions.

"She practically kissed me on the shuttle," I brag. "It was our cover, but still."

"*Practically*, but not *actually*." His judgment supersedes my arrogance. He won this round.

"I'm about to be married, Filip." I attempt to cover. "It wouldn't do for an engaged man to be kissing a girl who isn't his betrothed."

"That is a good point, Your Highness." He's back to being all business.

"Besides, Filip, I wasn't worried—I knew you were tracking me." I grin, tapping the small button on the breast pocket of my coat.

"Wouldn't have found you so quickly if I hadn't," he reminds me. I complain enough about technology tracking my every move in the palace that Filip is accustomed to my gripes. He relishes the moments when I actually appreciate his devices.

"We appreciate your assistance, miss," Filip says to Cindrill as we return. He bows his head slightly to her.

"Cindrill needs her arm looked at—she's been injured," I announce to the group. The men all eye her.

"I'm fine, I just need to get home to do my chores."

"I insist." I push. Taking hold of her uninjured arm, I wheel her around. "You'll like the palace—it's lovely there —and we'll send for your father so he can come and visit before collecting you to take you home. I'm sure there is a reward for saving the Prince of Davengreen."

"I don't think that's necessary," she argues.

"You can meet Vila since you seem so interested in her." I drop my voice. "Perhaps we can check her eye color together."

I wave everyone but Filip back from us. Two of the men walk ahead, the rest follow behind, though a few take the side streets, looking for any threats lurking in the shadows.

I glance up and notice the sky has taken a turn for the worse. Where there once were beautiful blue skies, there are now darker clouds—not enough to indicate a storm just yet, but enough to cast shadows over everything.

I replay the scene on the roof over again in my mind. Cindrill was fearless as she jumped from building to building—I wish I had the freedom to be fearless like her. Instead, I have responsibilities and duties.

Father will be furious when he finds out I jumped off a building. I can't say I blame him—under any other circumstances, it would be a stupid thing to do. Still, somehow, I have a feeling I'm going to tuck this one away as one of my favorite memories that I'll tell my children someday.

The group is quiet, falling into an awkward silence as we travel toward the town line to cross over into the palace district. Everyone takes turns glancing at Cindrill as we walk, but she keeps her eyes focused on the ground in front of her. Pebbles litter the path, and she kicks one as she walks.

Her boots peek out the front of her open skirt. Even outside of the palace, fashion is an important concept. The green detailing on her coat tells a story, I'm sure.

Cindrill looks ready to escape the first chance she gets, but her eyes are drilling holes into the ground before every step. Her nose is slanted just enough to turn up at the end, but her curls fall to the sides of her face, blocking it from my sight for most of the walk.

We're a block away from the town line, surrounded by large buildings that look as if they house machinery when a door flies open and Cindrill is pulled inside.

CHAPTER 7
CINDRILL

L arge hands clamp over my mouth as I'm pulled
from the side. Master's familiar scent fills my
nose, and I relax as he pulls me through the
building backward.

I assume the plan is to make it look like I was
abducted, and the prince won't be able to find me after
his guards race him back to the palace to protect him. If
we hurry, perhaps we can catch them as they are entering
the palace and slip in that way.

We make it five feet before the door bursts open
behind us and Davian storms in looking ready to murder
Master—an ironic twist.

He rushes toward us, carelessly leaving his guards
behind. His friend rushes after him, but not close enough
to catch the angry royal. Davian navigates around boxes

and wooden crates as he hurries toward us, intent on reaching me.

The prince threatens Master as he pulls me away to which Master just laughs. It's that dark, terrifying sound he produces when he's about to deliver someone's fate and he wants to terrorize them first. Davian doesn't seem to notice as he barrels toward us.

"Let me go," I insist, twisting against Master. Either way, it doesn't matter—stay with Master and go after the prince another day, or end up in the palace and gather intelligence from inside, possibly even letting Master in during the middle of the night to carry out his task of murdering the king and his son.

"Let her go, she has no part in this!" Davian shouts, leaping over a smaller crate, cutting off a few feet between us. He looks wild as he tries to reach me.

The prince slams into a different box, and I know his shin must be killing him, but that doesn't stop him. He lifts a small wooden container and throws it so that it smashes on the ground next to us—a warning.

"Release her, and I'll consider letting you live!" Davian sounds almost cocky as he wields his threats against the deadliest force Davengreen has ever been subjected to—this lifetime or any other.

"Go back to your palace, *boy,*" Master says, his voice modulator activated. If I didn't know the science behind it, I'd find it terrifying. I myself rather enjoy using the voice modulator Claude designed for us during my own missions.

Master pulls back on me, cutting off part of my airflow. My training tells me to escape—flip him over my head, incapacitate him, and run—but I know better, and tamp down years of experience in order to play the role of a victim.

A sound squeaks out of my mouth involuntarily, and my eyes widen when I hear it. On occasion, I don't have control over what my body does, and I hate it—I should be able to be flawless according to my level of training, but every so often, I find a crack in the perfect façade Master and the others have created in me.

Prince Davian looks ready to hit the floor, frozen, when he hears me make that ridiculous noise, making me sound like a frightened mouse. I growl, frustrated with myself, and it only spurs the prince on.

Filip races behind him, unable to catch him as he plows after me through the crowded room. I have no idea how Master can navigate the old factory backward, but I assume he scoped it out before we arrived.

Light shifts in my peripheral vision as Master weaves us around old boxes. The windows are boarded up, but not well, leaving light to leak in at strange angles. Dust dances in the air, puffing up in large clouds with each scuffled step we take.

I work to maneuver against Master, ensuring it

appears as though I'm trying to escape. Davian never takes his eyes off me, while Filip keeps his eyes locked on Master. One of Davian's men bursts through the back door faster than Master had anticipated and his grip tightens around my body, forcing the air from me just enough to let me know his plan was thrown off, but not enough for the prince or his men to tell he was surprised.

Davian reaches into his coat, retrieving the medical kit he had used not too long ago. I squint in question. Before I can figure it out, Davian whips his hand into the air and launches the kit directly at me.

It sails by my face, a mere inch from my temple and hits Master's cheekbone. He growls viciously as one of Davian's men yells behind him.

Now or never—flee and find me later or keep me in his grip and be overtaken by the king's men. Master could easily take out the majority of them, but he has a plan to think about, and Master always carries out his missions. I feel his thoughts trickling down to his fingers against my body as he makes his decision.

He releases me, pretending like Davian's assault mattered. He turns, forcing the air around me to gust like a sudden wind overtook the room. Master scrambles over something behind me, turning it in the process. It clinks against the floor, leaving the scene behind my back to my imagination.

Ahead of me, Davian falls.

Filip yells a string of threats against Master as he rushes to Davian's side, lifting a heavy box off of him.

"Wait, I'm coming," I shout as Filip tries to rock the large crate off of the prince's leg. The rest of the guards rush upstairs after Master—if he's on the second floor, they'll never catch him before he leaps from a window to freedom. "Tip it that way."

Filip and I work together to free the prince—I have no idea how Master lifted such a heavy box, but I'm sure adrenaline had something to do with it. Reeling back, I kick it, using my full weight to help assist the prince's friend.

The box topples over as Davian groans. His leg is still intact and doesn't appear to be out of the socket, but it has to hurt. I'm sure he will end up with some nasty bruises after this.

He and his father might be a matching set.

"It's fine," Davian protests as Filip tries to examine him. "It didn't even rip the fabric."

"It's going to bruise," I point out.

"I'm fine," Davian says harshly. He softens as he looks up at me. "How are *you*? Are *you* okay, Cindrill?"

A hand reaches out to me—to *point?...to ask me to come closer?...to help him up?* I'm not sure. No matter what his intent, I need to use it to my advantage.

I take his hand and settle on the floor in front of him, his legs still trailing behind him as he rests his full weight on his right hip. My skirt settles out to the side, and I position my legs out, mirroring his, but to the side instead of mostly behind me.

"I'm okay." My words are soft and quiet.

"Did he hurt you?" Davian covers my hand with his free one.

"I'm fine."

"I'm so sorry you got caught up in this, Cindrill. It wasn't fair of me to bring you into this and make you a target."

I was always *involved in this.*

The prince looks concerned, brow low. He ignores Filip's pleas to get up and move to safety. When the man tugs on Davian's shoulder, the prince swats him back, refusing to be deterred.

"I'll see to it that you're protected."

"I can take care of myself, Your Majesty."

Davian smirks. "I thought I told you not to call me that."

"I'll be fine," I insist.

"Your Highness, we need to go. Now," Filip finally demands.

I start to get up, pulling Davian with me. He hesitates for a moment, and I wonder if he wants to hold me in place a minute longer—the pressure on my hands suggests he might.

"You need to return to the palace where it's safe,

Davian, and I need to get home." I try to coax him to follow Filip's orders.

"We'll bring your father to the palace, Cindrill. Until we catch this madman, the safest place for you is with my guards."

He stands, leg not cooperating with him as he moves. The prince tumbles forward, only catching himself on Filip's outstretched arm.

I rush forward, ducking under his far arm as Filip takes on the majority of the prince's weight. Davian leans heavily against me, but I can tell he's trying not to. His muscles are tight, and he shifts toward Filip, allowing him to discretely take on more of the work.

Wrapping my arm around Davian's back, I brush against Filip's arm, but he doesn't flinch, holding the prince up. He makes it look easy—Filip is better at this than I thought.

"I'm fine," Davian mumbles. We wheel around toward the door as the rest of the guards join us, shaking their heads in a silent report.

"You threw a medical kit at an assassin," I comment. I probably should have picked that up. One of the guards goes back to get it as I wrench my head around to look for it. "You have pretty good aim for a sheltered royal."

"What do you think I do inside the palace walls all day?" he jokes back.

"I distinctly remember nearly being a victim several

times," Filip mumbles next to us as we step out onto the street.

The sky is still clear, the air crisp. Despite what was nearly carnage inside the old factory, the day has remained glorious outside.

"I threw it *near* you, Filip. It was just a wakeup call. If I had meant to hit you, I would have."

"I'm sure," Filip grumbles, and I gather Davian's wakeup calls were more frequent than they should have been.

Nanobots slowly start crawling up my skin, making their way to my neck. Quietly, I reach up to touch the spot. I hadn't realized it, but when my fingertip comes away red, I know I've been injured. Master's nail must have cut into me during the escape. The nanobots quickly cover up the injury, and I wipe the blood off on the dark fabric of my pants under my wrap skirt. At least if it blends in, Claude won't be able to yell at me for it.

The prince tries to walk on his leg, grimacing each time he puts weight on the injury. Our pace is slower than it should be if an assassin was on our trail, but Master isn't going to try anything else until we get back to the palace, so I let Filip take the lead in directing our pace without commenting on the situation.

Davian's men form a shield around us, moving us through the streets until we reach one of the shuttles.

The guards commandeer the vehicle, clearing a car before allowing us to enter.

I sit across from Davian, his legs kicked out as far as they'll reach toward me. I stay curled in on myself, tucking my legs under my seat. He watches me as we travel. Once, his eyes gaze toward the corner before snapping back to me—a silent reminder of earlier.

Strange. He's more resilient than I assumed he would be. He took on an assassin, didn't fuss over his injuries, and even has the gall to try to silently joke with me, drawing us back to our earlier moments on the shuttle.

Filip engages him in conversation and the two quietly discuss what to do to protect the Davengreen royals, Princess Vila, me, and the rest of the kingdom. Davian seems more worried about the kingdom at large than he does about what happens inside of the palace—with the exception of protecting Vila and me, that is.

He truly believes he is to blame for my involvement in all this.

"We should continue looking for the girl," Filip announces. "She can lead us to the man."

"Or men," I comment flippantly. "Could that *really* have been the same man all those times?"

"Well, it certainly couldn't have been the girl," Davian responds. "She hasn't been seen since the ball."

My eyebrows shoot up. "So it *was* a ball!"

Davian smirks at the triumph written on my face—

why try to hide it?

"You said it too many times," he protests playfully. "I picked up your word for it."

"You can't take it back, Your Highness." I purse my lips and shake my head playfully, pointing at him. "You said it and you can't retract it—this isn't the media. You don't control me; I heard you say it."

He closes his eyes slowly, shaking his head. He allows me this small dig against his family.

"Are you sure you're okay, Cindrill? He really didn't hurt you?"

My skin pings under the weight of his words, my neck throbbing just long enough to remind me that I'm a deceitful liar.

"I'm fine, I promise."

"We'll have the physician check you out just the same," Davian announces.

"I really need to go home now—"

"The prince saved your life, madam, you'll do as he says," Filip says abruptly. We both turn to stare.

"She could have handled herself, Filip," Davian corrects.

"Then why did you go running in after her?" The confrontation escalates even though their voices drop.

"It's my fault she's in this mess."

"Any of us could have gone after her." Filip raises a single eyebrow at his charge.

"You wouldn't have. You would have stayed and protected me."

"He makes a valid point, Filip," I add. "But please, can't I just go home?"

My words are only for show. I'll be more of a help to Master in the palace. *Won't I?*

Davian *had* saved me though. He risked himself to run in after me, full well knowing that an assassin who had nearly shot him off a roof just a little while earlier was holding me captive. The prince had even endured being injured to try to help me.

I wonder if there is a way to kill the king but leave his son to rule. Master hadn't told me the full contents of the missive with directions for the mission, but I know the king was supposed to be taken out so that someone else could ascend the throne...that meant Davian had to die too. The king had to go first, though.

I wonder if Claude would be able to get me more information. Master often tells him less than me—he doesn't need to know what I know—but what he tells him is usually different information than mine, so on the rare occasion we can speak in private, we've been able to piece together more parts of different missions than Master would like. I wish I knew more about reprograming nanobots—maybe I could reach out to him and uncover a way to save Davian.

The shuttle screeches to a stop, jerking quickly. I

nearly topple off my seat, too busy thinking about changing the plans to pay attention to our movements. The guards stand quickly, preparing to clear the area before we step out.

The doors open to reveal the same Epicenter we left a few hours ago. As if we were still there, I can see where each of us stood before being pushed into the shuttle. Davian steps out first, offering me his hand.

I take it and walk out onto the platform. Knowing I have to protect myself once I set foot inside the palace, I force each step to connect with the Epicenter floors hard enough to produce a sound, leaving my boots to click. It echoes off the walls like some of the fancy shoes the ladies of the court often wear to the balls and palace events. If it's annoying enough now, the guards will remember it later when I'm sneaking around the palace to let Master in. They'll be less likely to catch me because they'll be listening for the clicking sounds that won't be there later as I move.

Stomping isn't pleasant, but if it gets the job done, I'll act like one of those lumbering fools that thought they could make the cut with Master last year. Walking on the dirt will muffle the sound anyway, so I only have to keep it up until we leave the Epicenter. I can start again once I'm in the palace walls.

Davian keeps pace next to me, telling me all about the palace as we vacate the Epicenter.

CHAPTER 8
DAVIAN

"I thought I sent you to find an assassin," my father growls as I enter the office. His leg is bandaged, but I can see the tiniest hint of blood peeking through the wrap.

"I found him several times," I reply boldly. "Apprehending him was another matter."

He catches sight of Cindrill behind me and sits upright.

"Is this the girl?" he nearly shouts, looking ready to behead her on the spot.

"No!" I shout louder than I mean to. I quiet my voice, knowing I need to approach the matter gently if I want Cindrill to remain in the palace walls without giving away too many details about the day. "She was questioned this morning, but the shoe didn't fit. She presented several skills I thought could be useful to my search, and given her gender, I assumed she could calm the rest of the women we were questioning and set them at ease so we didn't cause a scene."

"Why is she here?" Father tips his chin up, examining her from the dark oak chair with intricate carvings at the head of the table. Papers lay spread out before him, several pens strewn around. It amazes me that he insists on using such an antiquated way of taking notes and ruling his kingdom, but I'll have my own ways when I'm king.

"We were both injured by the assassin. We've returned to regroup, go through the security footage of the towns to try to track him, and to have the girl examined by the physician at my command."

Cindrill cringes next to me. I can't imagine she's pleased with being spoken about like this, but at least she's not stepping out of line in front of my father.

"Hmm." His snort means he wants full details on Cindrill once she's not in the room with us. At this point, I'm not sure I want to tell him of Cindrill's particular skills—she may not ever be able to leave our employ if he finds her useful, and I could never knowingly trap her here. I'll have to stay by her side until I can get her out of the palace.

"Filip will help us to the infirmary so the physicians

can check us over. Once we've looked through the footage from today, I'll report back with our plan."

I turn, trying not to hobble as I walk to the door, the others following me. My leg has become easier to walk on, but I'm still limping a bit.

"Check on Vila," Father's voice calls after me. "Assure her that she's safe."

He makes a good point.

I raise a hand to indicate I've heard him and continue into the hallway. One of the men shuts the door behind us and I relax. Cindrill's hand brushing against mine pulls me right back out of the feeling.

"Blue, you said?" she asks.

It takes a moment for me to understand, but then I nod. Vila's eyes are blue—they have to be.

"I'll take you to meet my fiancée," I instruct loud enough for everyone to hear. "Huston, go get Sturges and tell him to meet us in the infirmary. We're not going to waste time sending this through the chain—he can tell us all at once what he's learned."

Filip clenches his jaw but doesn't argue.

Cindrill looks like she's taking in every bit of the palace, from the ornately decorated hallways to the massive tapestries she catches sight of through the open doorways. I wonder what she'll think of the ballroom when she sees it later.

"It's a bit much, don't you think?" she comments quietly.

"It's not as bad as you think," I reply, running a hand through my hair. "It wasn't all done at once. This is a cumulation of bits and pieces of every ruler since the beginning of the dynasty. We all get to add our own touches, and over the years, this is what it's become."

"Even the sons and daughters that did not inherit the crown were given a chance to add their marks," Filip adds, sounding almost as proud as my family is of the tradition. "While the palace has many ways of making income, the majority of it goes right back into the kingdom—that's why we don't always have as much money as we need when things come up. It's also why our enemies think they can so easily take over here."

"It's why we've had some of the recent taxes. We've been having some trouble with some of our neighboring countries and need extra money to help secure the borders." I lean toward Cindrill. "We've been trying to keep it quiet so we didn't upset everyone, but there have been some issues along the borders that we've been keeping isolated."

She nods. I hope I'm not scaring her too much.

The men stop around us, allowing me to step up to Vila's chambers. Cindrill stays by Filip's side as Vila's herald disappears into her sitting room to announce me.

After a moment, he reappears, holding his arm out to invite me in.

Stepping inside, I find the room bathed in firelight. Natural light streams in the windows, but the roaring faux fire consumes the colors, turning them orange. Vila strides across the room, hands folding into one another in front of her.

She blinks, waiting for me to speak.

"Are you well?" I ask quietly, reaching for her hands.

"I'm fine. You?" Her eyes are downcast. I can't quite see their color. Cindrill will destroy me if I've guessed incorrectly.

"Look at me, Vila." I have to know.

Hazel. Cindrill will be merciless.

Vila sighs. "What is it, Davian?"

"You're safe here, Vila. You know that, right?" I don't know her well, but I know I don't want her to live in fear in my home.

"I do," she agrees dutifully.

"We went after the assassin today," I inform her, still holding her hands. "We nearly had him, but he took a captive. We all managed to escape, but *he* also managed to flee. We're tracking him down right now."

"Who is *she*?" Vila nods toward Cindrill, whispering her words. A blonde strand of hair falls with the movement.

"She is part of my team. She was assisting me today

when we ran into the assassin."

"Why is she here?" Vila ducks her head closer to me, clearly offended.

"We were both injured today during the fights—"

"*Fights?* Plural?" She forgets to keep her voice low.

"We escaped the assassin once, but he found us a second time. I insisted Cindrill return with us so that the physician could check her over before we return her to her father."

"How did you say she helped you?"

I try not to grin. "We might have had to jump off a building to escape, and she made sure we didn't die in the process."

"*Davian.*" I can't tell if it's shock or a lecture.

"We're both fine, we just need to be examined quickly."

Vila waves her hand as if I should move. When I don't, she puts a hand on her hip. "Let's go. If you need to be examined, we'll continue this conversation in the infirmary."

"You don't have to come with—"

"Oh, yes I do. And even if I didn't, Davengreen and Briarmar are supposed to be united. We can't act as one if one of us is constantly being left out of the loop. Harold, you're in charge while I'm gone."

A herald named Harold…I should have seen that coming. Cindrill eyes me as I walk by her, smirking. She must have seen the surprise written across my features when I discovered my fiancée's staff's name.

The infirmary is a few degrees cooler than the rest of the palace. Cindrill is settled in a station two away from mine, giving me some privacy. Vila quickly follows behind her.

"That can't be good," Filip mumbles, taking a seat off to the side.

"Your Highness," Sturges interrupts. He holds up a tablet. "The video from today, sire."

Once again, we discover that the assassin knew where all the cameras were and managed to hide from most of them. He looks tall and imposing in the flashes we catch, covered in dark clothing.

"Did you?" Vila's voice rises up, sounding shocked. We all look over, but the curtain blocks our line of sight.

"You're going to regret letting that happen," Filip taunts, pointing to the two women.

"Something I should know?" Dr. Romani asks as he slides his hand along my leg checking for injuries. He's been caring for my family for the last decade and likes to joke around with me when my father isn't present. He more than anyone helped me through losing my mother, acting both as a doctor and as a therapist.

"It's a good thing the prince has a strong sense of duty, that's all I can say," Filip jokes.

"That pretty girl you brought in?" Dr. Romani jabs at what will likely be a nasty bruise tomorrow. "She's rather beautiful, no?"

"No!"

I protested too much. They all look at me, eyebrows raised.

Grumbling internally, I quickly search for an excuse for my outburst.

"I have a beautiful fiancée," I remind them. "I thought Cindrill could be useful as a spy, but now I'm not sure."

"Ah," Dr. Romani offers. "You don't want her to be trapped here."

Ten years of listening to me complain about being trapped in the palace, and suddenly the man thinks he knows how I think. He pauses his examination to ask a few questions.

"So, you don't want this girl to be trapped here. That's wise of you to protect her," he continues once I've answered about my pain level.

"There's no reason for her to work for us. She worked for us today and nearly ended up dead twice in a matter of the few hours she's been with me."

"And nearly ended up destroying your marriage, so I hear." Filip chuckles, knowing he can trust both Dr. Romani and Sturges. He wouldn't speak out of turn if anyone else had been close enough to overhear and risk the union.

"Oh?" Dr. Romani says, amused. "Your leg is fine, Davian. Put some ice on it and don't overextend yourself, but you shouldn't have any lasting issues. It will be sore tomorrow though."

"Thanks," I reply, hoping he doesn't press further about the scene on the shuttle.

"Is he finished yet?" Vila asks suddenly from nearby. Filip tugs the curtain back, revealing her. "Cindrill is fine."

Both women stand next to the curtain wall, waiting for us. Vila looks ready to move on, but Cindrill's lips are tight.

"How, precisely, are we spending the rest of our day?" Vila asks. I've noticed she likes to keep to a schedule.

I imagine with a lecture or two.

"Perhaps a tour?" Cindrill suggests suddenly.

"Yes, why don't you give Cindrill a tour, Vila?"

She looks uncomfortable. "Why don't *you* guide us, Davian?"

Vila must not be comfortable enough with the palace layout yet to give a guest a tour. Dr. Romani hands me a few pills to take, and the pain eases immediately.

"Of course," I nod to my bride-to-be. Holding out my arm to her, I wait for her to take it.

The palace seems twice as big as usual, and I've only taken the girls to a few of the more important areas, explaining the history. In between locations, Sturges and Filip review what we know about the assassin, the girls taking a particular interest.

Eventually, we find ourselves in my study, making a plan of action. The light outside wanes, leaving us in a muddled cross between natural light and artificial illumination. It's that strange time of day when everything looks a little off in the mixture of light.

Vila and Cindrill bend over tablets together, swiping through footage of the assassin and talking about how he knew to avoid the cameras. I watch them in a trance until Filip kicks me under the table.

"And you said he was *here* last night, too, right?" Cindrill comments, not looking up from the tablet. "And he avoided the camera then, too?"

"He had to have access to the palace schematics," Filip replies. "We keep those under lock and key, no one should be able to discover the ins and outs of the palace unless they work here."

"You think it was an inside job?" Cindrill sounds surprised, finally looking up.

"We don't know," I offer. "How else would he know how to move, though?"

"And the woman?"

"She had the most beautiful outfit," Vila jumps in. "Even her shoes were perfect."

"I took care of those," I mumble. She looks at me sharply. I quickly explain how I cut the girl and marked up the shoes, earning myself a dissatisfied huff.

"The girl shoved me in a closet to protect me, so she can't be all that bad," Vila protests.

"And she tried to assassinate *my* father and me, so she can't be that *good* either." I watch her to gauge her reaction. Vila may not love me, but if she wishes the assassin succeeded, I'll be able to catch her.

"True." She sighs. "Maybe we can reason with her though if it comes to it. Perhaps she'll turn on the man if we catch her.

Filip looks like he wants to ask how she proposes to do that, but then realizes she is not our friend yet and he can't speak bluntly to her. He closes his mouth without speaking.

"Thoughts on how to do that?" Cindrill asks instead, taking a genuine interest in what Vila has to say. "Have those hazel eyes of yours spotted something the rest of us haven't?"

The emphasis on Vila's eye color is a direct slap in the face to me as Cindrill flashes her gaze up at me. She's proven her point.

A knock sounds at the door. Sturges stands to open it.

"The king would like to see you," a voice says. We've wasted several hours since returning, and I'm sure he's not happy I haven't spoken with him yet.

"Why don't you ladies come with me?"

"I sincerely doubt your father wants to see me right now," Cindrill replies, glancing up. "Take your fiancée, though, he's less likely to be mad in her presence. She has a calming effect on people from what I've seen."

Cindrill glances back down while Vila beams. Perhaps the two of them could be friends.

"I'll come. I'm sure by now he's heard from my father, and I'll have to do some damage control anyway." Vila walks over to stand alongside of me. "I suppose that's both of our jobs now."

"Will you be okay, Cindrill?" I ask.

She barely looks up, waving us off with a flick of her fingers. Sturges stays in place while Filip and most of the others rise to walk with us. Cindrill makes a small noise, a dismissal of sorts. When I stand there a moment longer, she glances up.

"I'll be fine," she finally responds. "I'm just going to keep studying these. There has to be something we're missing."

I have no doubt if we've missed anything, she'll be the one to find it.

CHAPTER 9
CINDRILL

Sturges eyes me from across the table but goes about his work, studying footage. Now that I'm basically alone on this side of the study, I can break into the system and cover my tracks. Vila is a sharp one and probably would have caught me if I had tried to reach out to Claude while she was sitting next to me.

My fingers slowly move over the keyboard so my guard doesn't notice, hacking into the system like Claude taught me to do. I don't have time to tell him about the shoes he made me, but I have to make sure he's alone before I tell him what I really need.

It takes a few moments—longer than I'd like—to get into his system and get him to notice my quiet appearance on the screen in his basement workroom where he creates wardrobe and gadgets for Master's missions.

When I finally get his attention, he sends me a message back asking where I am.

Once he's confirmed he's alone using a special signal we created, I tell him as much as I can get away with typing. If Sturges wasn't as mindful as Filip, I might have been able to get away with more, but sadly, he's just as keen.

Each word is painfully slow to type. Each reply is lengthy and makes the situation more bearable. Claude has been with Master longer than I have, but we truly only have each other. As uppity as Claude can be, he needs me as much as I need him.

Claude tells me everything he knows and informs me he's snooping in the bunker for more information about who hired Master and me to kill the King and Prince of Davengreen. I don't hold out much hope, but he sends me messages, keeping me informed of what he's doing. I watch them scrawl across the side of the screen while I search for Master's travels in the time since we separated—I know his many nanobot faces and have a better chance of identifying him on my own.

"Do you have access to any other cameras?" I ask, knowing Sturges is likely watching everything on my screen on his own device—good thing he can't see Claude's program on the edge of my tablet.

"Just this," he mumbles.

My name pings on the screen as Claude responds to me, drawing my attention. I wait for him to continue.

"It was her father."

The halls are dimly lit as everyone escorts me to my room for the evening. I put up a fuss about bringing my father to the palace, only to be answered with grumblings about trying to locate him.

Is Vila in on this? How much does she know about her father's plan?

We pause at her room as she volunteers to give me something to wear to bed. I slip in after her, passing by Harold who is still standing watch over the doorway.

Inside, her own people hover about, dipping into curtseys when they notice their princess gliding across the room. She smiles kindly at them and guides us to her walk-in closet. Layers of pastel-colored dresses fill the space. Shoes are quietly lined up on the floor under them, save for those in the massive cubbies at the end of the closet. Scarves hang down on one side, belts and wraps hang on the other. A set of drawers reveal a massive amount of jewelry.

"Gifts from Davengreen, mostly. I left the majority of my jewels at home until after the wedding. Daddy will send the rest of my belongings over then." She waves her hand at the glittering jewels.

"You weren't sure this was going to work?" I ask. Vila looks back at me as if I've said something wrong.

"I'm sure you know it's an arranged marriage, Cindrill. I'm doing this for the honor of my father and country, but Daddy would never force me to marry a man who was cruel to me. I'm here to make sure I won't be mistreated in the future, but the rest of my things will be sent along once we've said our vows."

"A quick exit if need be; it makes sense." I run my fingers over a necklace. Claude would have a field day ripping these apart and transforming them. "Do you plan to leave, Vila?"

In the several hours we've known each other, I can pretend we've become friends. Perhaps she'll play along out of propriety.

"I've found Prince Davian to be a good and kind man. I don't know him well, but I'm not afraid of him." She turns her back to me, rummaging through a drawer.

"You're sure he's kind?" I continue to muse, fingering the lace on the sleeve of a deep red dress, one of the few that isn't pastel.

"I believe him to be, yes. He seems kinder than his father, at least." The Princess of Briarmar turns back to me, straightening her shoulders. "I'm going to marry him, Cindrill, if that's what you're asking. He's made a commitment to *me*, and he will honor that, just as *I* will honor my commitment to *him*."

She thinks I'm angling for her to leave so I can have the prince.

"I'm glad to hear that. I think you'll be good for the future of our kingdom. I like that you're here, Vila." My words seem to set her at ease slightly. She hands me a set of light pink silk pajamas. "Thank you."

There's no way I'm taking my clothes off knowing that Master will be here to finish his mission tonight, but I take the garments to complete the act. I haven't been stomping around this palace all evening for nothing.

How much about this assassination do you know, Vila?

She smiles stiffly and nods. When I remove the silk pajamas the rest of the way from her hands, her smile fades into a genuine one. "The men will see you to your room. If there's anything you need, just ask."

My room isn't nearly as large as Vila's, but it's spacious enough that I don't know how I could ever fall asleep. My tiny room in Master's bunker is comforting—I know every inch of it. This is too grand, too open, too unknown.

As soon as I'm alone, I turn out the lights and search for a way out of the room. No panels shift on the walls, no closets give way to hidden hallways, nothing under the plush rug moves to reveal a hidden staircase. My only option is the window.

Stepping outside into the cool night air, the wind snaps against me. I draw my hood up over my hair and tuck the loose strands back so they don't whip in my face.

The roof is slanted, but the shingles offer a little resistance, and I'm able to make my way down a few rooms. I check each carefully before passing the window, simultaneously checking behind me to ensure no one on the ground is watching me.

The fourth window away offers me my best chance. I pry it open, using the nanobots as a pick. It pops open in my hand, and I quietly slip into the dark room.

The moon is high enough to offer a soft, glowing light in the room, just enough to see by now that my eyes have adjusted to being outside. I move slowly, trying not to run into anything.

If Vila's father ordered the hit on the king and his son, I need to find out why, but more than that, I need to see if Vila has anything to do with this. Master will be waiting for a signal from me, but I can put it off a little while longer, even if he *did* witness me crawling across the palace roof.

The door is quiet as I open it. I watch the men outside my door for a few minutes, waiting for a pattern in their movements. They spend most of their time watching their tablets, but they pause every two minutes to look down both sides of the hallway. I duck back inside the room as they glance my way.

When they turn to see the right side of the hall, I make my move, darting out into the hallway and throwing myself against the wall in the connecting passageway. When I don't hear anything, I risk a glance—the men haven't noticed me.

Turning back, I walk down the hall. In the wing with the study, I overhear the guards discussing the king setting up shop in the ballroom for the evening with his son. I adjust my pack on my shoulder and head toward the ballroom.

I consider using the nanobots to shield my face, but if I'm caught, I can claim I was just trying to go home to my father. If they catch me as another person, I'll have no way of explaining myself out of the situation.

I consider my options as I traipse through the palace halls. I could kill the king. Once it's done, if I flee and leave Davian to take over his father's reign, surely Master won't be able to finish the job—Claude said it had to be done the same night for it to work. The king dies, followed immediately by his son—I suppose so Vila would officially take control at that point as the next in line after her husband...or husband-to-be. The guards won't leave the prince alone if his father dies and nothing happens to Davian immediately.

I could let Master in and obstruct his ability to hurt Davian. Maybe I could hide him somewhere off the palace grounds and release him when it's safe. Master would never think to look in any of his own hiding places for the escaped prince of Davengreen.

I can hear the prince and his father talking from outside of the ballroom. The sounds drift down the hallway gently, as soft as the glow of the chandeliers. I'm on the lower level, knowing it will be easier to spy if I'm not at the top of a staircase, but it's a strange feeling to enter without descending the stairs.

Davian and his father sit on their thrones at the far end of the ballroom, leaning in toward each other to talk and point at pieces of paper. Davian holds a tablet in his hands, the blue glow bouncing off his light shirt. He's removed his dark waistcoat, and I almost miss the sight of it.

"What are you doing here?" a voice hisses behind me.

I spin, ready to attack, but Vila grabs my hood and drags me backward, away from the ballroom, choking me slightly.

"Let me go," I hiss, batting at her.

"Why are you here?"

"I was trying to leave."

"Through the ballroom?" she confronts me.

"I don't know how to get around here," I seethe.

"You managed to get past the guards just fine," she

points out. "Why are you here, Cindrill?"

Her voice is cold, and I'm certain she knows of her father's plot. He wants the throne of Davengreen, and if his daughter is the widowed princess, she'll be in control here, reverting power to him. There's no way she doesn't know about this—why else would she follow me?

"Why are you stalking me?"

"I don't trust you," she admits forcefully, still holding her voice down so the king and prince don't hear us. "My country needs this marriage, and I won't let you ruin this for us."

"*Why* do you need this marriage?" I demand answers.

"We're having trouble on our borders. We need a stronger army. We need reinforcements." Vila's eyes hold that same look they did when she spoke about her orphanage.

What if she doesn't know, my thoughts whisper. No, *she has to—her father is trying to steal an entire kingdom.*

"So, out of the goodness of your heart, you're marrying the prince so you can gain access to his armies?"

"And he's doing the same for our money…and men. There's war all around, Cindrill—I don't know if you've noticed or not, but people are dying and we're trying to save them."

"How exactly do you expect to save both countries, Vila?" I demand, circling her. She made the wrong choice engaging with me, and if it comes down to it, I'll take her out right now. "If you're pulling men from Davengreen to protect Briarmar, who will defend Davengreen?"

"We'll take turns assisting each other," she protests, huffing. Her hands clench at her sides as she realizes I'm moving around her, corralling her away from the throne room. If I can lock her in another closet until this is over, I might use that option. "Right now, the threat is greater for Briarmar, and we've got money we can give to Davian and his father."

Her voice rises in pitch with every word, suddenly worried. I'm not quite as nice as she thought I was, though, she also believes I was trying to steal her fiancé.

"I will not allow you to steal Davian away and crush my kingdom." She tries to be brave.

"I'm not stealing your fiancé, Vila. That's not why I'm here." I glare at her. "You've got two options: get in a closet and stay there until I tell you otherwise or die right now."

"You won't hurt me."

"I will," I assure her. I take a menacing step toward her. Footsteps sound behind me—the king and prince must have figured out we were out here and are coming to investigate.

I whip around, looking over my shoulder to check, but when I do, Vila lashes out, grabbing at me. She manages to spin me enough that my bag falls off my shoulder. I pull back on it in response. The shoe bounces out as the bag crashes against the floor.

Kicking out, I swipe her legs from under her. She hits the floor hard, letting out a sharp cry. The men run faster, coming to her aid, but they still have half the ballroom to traverse before reaching us—they can't tell who we are yet.

Grabbing the shoe, I pull her arm, forcing her up. She stumbles as I drag her away, tucking the shoe back in my bag.

"Make one sound and I'll make sure your jaw is wired shut for at least a month," I threaten, holding my elbow ready to strike back into her face as we run. My far hand stretches across my chest, biting into the flesh on her upper arm.

"I was kind to you," she whispers, hissing at me.

"And I was to *you*." She has no way of knowing I saved her, though. Not yet.

I'm faster than the king and his son, giving us an exceptional lead on what was already a very strong head start. I race us around corners until it will be hard to find us. Still, then men press forward, yelling for guards.

"Let go of me, Cindrill." Her words are laced with venom.

"You don't get to hurt the prince tonight, Vila. You and your father will never get away with this."

"What are you talking about?" She claws at my arm

and I shoulder-check her into a wall for good measure. She cries out. "We haven't done anything—"

"You put a hit out on the king and his son!" I shout. I didn't mean to be so loud. Then again, I also didn't mean to care at all. My job is to kill them, after all. Vila is just the one that hired us.

"We did no such thing!" Vila shouts, prying at my fingers once again.

"Your father hired an assassin to kill the king, followed by your precious husband-to-be. Don't tell me you didn't know."

Vila freezes. I'm jerked to a stop.

Her face is tight with shock. Her eyes twitch back and forth as if she's reading a tablet, trying to process everything. I see the moment she realizes what her father has done, her eyes snapping up to look at me.

"He couldn't," she whispers.

"He did." My words are harsh and uncaring. She needs me to be gentle as her world falls apart, but I refuse to be.

"My father wouldn't—" Tears fall down her face. "No, he wouldn't."

"Vila, either you knew, or he lied to you too, but either way, your father will pay for this. Now I need to know if *you* will too."

"I had no idea." Her whisper is soft as the footsteps get closer.

"Time to move." I grab her arm, forcing her along.

"How did you find out?" she asks. I don't answer. "Cindrill, how did you know? Are you protecting Davian? Why are you here?"

My eyes sweep the area, looking for somewhere to hide.

"If you don't answer me, I'll tell them everything!" she cries out.

"Why did your father hire an assassin? So you could rule once they were dead?" I shouldn't have pointed out her father's intentions given the disheveled state she's in, but I can't help but make the jab.

"Is that why you were trying to steal him away? Why are you so set on taking Davian for yourself?" she demands answers.

A loud explosion makes the ground beneath us rumble. Master has arrived.

"Get in there." I push her into a closet. "Stay quiet."

I realize too late that she's heard those words before. She looks at me in horror.

"You're here to kill him." Vila looks horrified, paling in the muted light from outside the closet.

"I'm not going to kill him." Her brows furrow, thinking. "I didn't hurt you, and I'm not going to hurt him."

A second, louder explosion knocks me off my feet. Master is serious this time.

"Go," Vila says, believing me.

I have one chance to stop this.

CHAPTER 10
DAVIAN

The lights twitch, blinking overhead. At least one of the bulbs is flickering on and off, hovering between life and death. I sit up, trying to figure out what's happening, but the chandelier crashes a few feet away, spewing glass everywhere.

Next to me, my father lays still, propped up against the wall. I shake him, and he groans.

"What happened?"

"There was an explosion."

"Where?" My father sits upright, more alert. Blood trickles from a cut on his temple where he hit the wall, but he seems to be okay other than that.

The scent of dust fills the air—the explosion couldn't have been too far away. The guards call our names.

"Here!" I shout, thinking it might not have been my best choice after the fact.

Filip rounds the corner with several men behind him.

"There's been a breach."

"Yes," a dark voice adds from down the hall. "There has."

The assassin.

Filip's face mirrors my own—covered in terror. Everyone grabs my father, forcing him to run as I stumble to my feet.

Two men run behind me—Filip and one of his team. They raise their weapons, holding their orders silent as we rush down the hall.

Splitting up, we follow procedure, ensuring at least one of us has a better chance of survival. The last I see of my father, he's stumbling down the left corridor toward a safe room hidden in one of the sitting rooms. My leg throbs, but I won't stop.

"Oh, Your Highness…" the assassin's voice calls, changing tones. He must be using some device to change what he sounds like as he taunts us.

I'm simultaneously relieved and horrified when he moves to the right, following us instead of my father.

"Go," Filip whispers harshly. "*Get there.*"

He doesn't use the words, afraid the assassin will hear, but he means for me to get to the infirmary where we've set up a blockade that should keep the assassin out. Inside the medical wing of the palace, we've got a secondary room, so even if he *can* breach the medical wing, he won't be able to get to me.

"*Don't*," I warn harshly. I know Filip will stay behind to try to stop him.

"Move," Filip directs.

"What about the girls? Cindrill and Vila?" I question, realizing I had been on my way to investigate whatever Vila was yelling about outside of the ballroom when the explosion rocked the palace.

"I'll find them."

"You'll be dead," I correct, reminding him he's about to try to take on a murderer we've been trying to escape since his first attempt on my life.

"Sturges will find them."

"Tell him," I insist, knowing Sturges will prioritize my father and I. Vila will be prioritized too as a foreign dignitary and the sole link to Briarmar and Davengreen's survival, but Cindrill will be on her own, once again because of me.

Filip taps his radio and relays my demands to his counterpart as the assassin picks up his pace. He's no longer trying to hide—he *wants* to terrorize us.

Ahead, Dr. Romani flings the door open to the infirmary and motions us forward silently. The men pull me forward, knowing I'm already trying to find a way out of the infirmary so I can find Cindrill and Vila and ensure they're safe.

"You too," Dr. Romani whispers after I'm pushed through the door. "You're the only one that can keep him in place in here."

Filip stumbles in behind me, crashing into my back as the doctor pulls him into the room, closing the door. My friend looks surprised when I wheel around to face him.

"Did you—?" He stumbles. "Did you just pull me in here?"

He whips around to glare at Dr. Romani.

"You would have died out there facing whatever you were running from alone—*I assume that assassin*—and we both know Davian would have tried to escape to save Cindrill again, so you tell me...should I have left you out there?"

Something slams against the door, leaving a dent in the metal. We jerk around to look.

He's approaching the infirmary.

Voices mumble outside the door. The girl is with him.

"The feeds," Filip mumbles, pushing me back. "Go to the room. I'll pull the feeds up."

I follow his commands, knowing that if both the assassin and the murderess are here with us, they aren't with my father, Cindrill, or Vila. We'll be protected locked in the safe room inside the bunker disguised as a medical wing, and keeping their attention here will give our men time to formulate a plan and take them down.

The screens in the room burst to life with a blue glow, quickly taking on the shapes of the hallways outside of us as Filip assesses the situation. He quickly calls back and forth to the security room as he coordinates a plan with our men.

I stare at the screen that shows the outside of the infirmary. The assassin is tall, covered in black clothing once again. He has a hood over his head, concealing him even when he *does* turn toward the camera.

A woman is standing next to him. Her clothes are strikingly similar to Cindrill's, but it's clearly not her face peeking out from under the hood. I'm terrified that she could have taken the garments from Cindrill—but then, Cindrill knows how to protect herself, and I see no tears in the fabric or blood on the cloth. Cindrill wouldn't have given up her clothing willingly, and with no sign of struggle, I can only assume she's fine and didn't encounter the assassin woman.

The two talk to each other for a moment before turning toward the door. The woman stands back as the man attempts to break in. He holds his arm out and something crawls off it.

"Filip!" I backhand him so hard he nearly drops his tablet as he jolts. Then I point. "That's what I saw!"

He stares at the screen hanging on the wall above us, leaning closer.

"What is that?"

"I don't know, but that's what happened to the assassin's face."

"What?" Dr. Romani demands, eyes wide as I turn to him.

"Her face..." I start. "When she was running away after shoving Vila in the closet...it shattered...or something, I don't know."

Our view is obscured, and I can't tell what is happening with the thing that crawled off the man's hand.

"Watch him." I direct the others as I latch on to the woman in the frame. There has to be *something* to help us.

Another man walks up to them—a third assassin. The lead man is taller and stronger looking, but this one sidles up to the woman and tips his head toward her, saying something.

After a moment, the door to the infirmary swings open as if the tall man hadn't had to lift a finger. Filip goes still next to me. "How is that possible?"

"They can get in here, can't they?" Dr. Romani voices the question we all have battling inside our heads. We're no longer safe in this fortress.

"We need a plan." Filip's words move us all into action.

On the screens, I catch sight of the assassins walking

toward us. They don't seem to care about the medical supplies laying around, they just search for where we might be hiding.

The woman ducks to look under every table and bed, trying quickly to keep up with the men, but the tall assassin doesn't seem concerned. It's almost as if he knows where we'll be.

His hand looks intact once more. Nothing appears to have changed, but we all saw it, didn't we?

Once again, I freeze, watching the woman—she seems to be the wildcard. If we can appeal to her senses, perhaps she'll side with us. She saved Vila and defied the man once before—maybe money would be a suitable reason to change her allegiances. I'm willing to try anything.

She ducks again, searching more frantically for us, but the man doesn't stop. "What are you doing?" I whisper.

"Trying to block the door," Filip replies, not realizing I'm speaking to the girl on the screen. "How about a little help, *Your Highness*?"

Right. Help.

I turn, rushing to the door the men are trying to brace.

"Sturges says your father is safe," Filip adds when I take a place by him.

"Any word on Vila and Cindrill?" I ask, hearing the frantic tone in my voice. I didn't mean to sound like that.

"Nothing yet, I'm afraid. I'm sure they're fine. The girl saved Vila before, so maybe she did it again."

"I hope."

A strange sound hums just above our voices and everyone freezes. The noise persists, but softer. It's enough to terrify us all. Whatever the assassin had done to open the infirmary doors, he was doing it again.

This time, on the screens, we can see it all. Some type of device crawls off the assassin and covers part of the door, moving like a silent wave as it changes the door. With each movement, the hum changes—the inner workings of the door bending to the will of the creature forcing its hand.

"They're bots," Filip whispers. "He has technology we barely have access to, Davian. Those are nanobots. No wonder he was able to get away with so much."

He shakes his head.

"We stay and fight; we give the prince a chance. Davian, you go out of the back entrance and get as far from the palace as you can. Go into hiding. Do whatever you need to do, but don't stay here. We'll hold him off."

"I can't—"

"Yes, you can, Davian. When he's done here, he's going after your father and we might not be able to stop him. You may be the only hope for the people at this point, and you might be the only one who can get away. You have to go. The second this door opens, you run, do you understand?"

Dr. Romani wheels around to face me. "He's right, lad. You have to go. We'll cover for you here, and we'll do our best to protect your father, but one of you has to survive this night. This is your job—your duty."

I nod. Leaving him behind will be like leaving a second father to be lost to the assassin. I have no choice but to do as he asks.

But first, I'll find Cindrill and Vila and take them with me.

The door creeks—it's nearly open. Filip and the others raise their weapons, prepared to fight. On the screen, the assassins raise their weapons too.

I wait by the hidden door, prepared to make my move. I make my peace with saying goodbye to my friends as they valiantly give the crown a chance to save the kingdom from this madman.

The moment the door opens, I escape out of the back. Shouts rise up behind me.

"Cindrill!" someone shouts. I wheel back around.

CHAPTER 11
CINDRILL

The nanobots on my face scurry away as Master forces the door open. I need them to know who I am, even if it means I'll be on the run for the rest of my life.

Waiting until the door starts to open, I hold my hands up where Master can't see me. Claude catches sight of me and nods, doing the same as he takes my side and backs me. Filip and the others have guns trained on us.

I know I'm signing my own death certificate, but the prince and his father shouldn't die because Briarmar's king wants to take power from them without starting a war—it will be easier to get Davengreen to cooperate if they think Vila is legally and rightfully in charge. Turning on Master is the worst thing I can do, but Davian is behind those men somewhere, and I don't want him to die tonight.

"Cindrill," Filip says loudly, shocked to see me. My nanobots congregate just below my collar, waiting for orders.

Master wheels around to me, driving the butt of his gun into my stomach. I keel over, thrown off by Filip's proclamation. I clutch at my abdomen, gasping for air. I've never been caught this off guard before with Master; at least, not since I was in training.

Claude looks like he wants to move toward me, but he doesn't dare with Master's anger lashing out like tentacles ready to slice us in half. Claude will support me, but he knows how to play the game.

Filip races forward, prepared to engage. I kick out, slamming into one of Master's boots. He stumbles forward just enough to knock his gun to tip down. It goes off, firing into a guard's leg. He screams in pain.

Master reels around, prepared to end me. Leaping to my feet, I strike. Behind Master, Filip and the others attack, trying to pull him from me.

I'm faster than anyone expected and slam into Master, ripping part of the nanobot mask from his face. The creatures blink bright blue where I tore them apart, more racing up to replace the ones I throw on the ground.

Claude gasps as I ruin his creation but uses the scene

to fuel him. He's not a fighter like I am, but he knows how to use his technology to his advantage. Using something on his wrist, he taps commands.

Master suddenly shouts in pain, frightening us all. With his voice modulator disabled, he sounds like himself. The nanobots retract from his face, taking pieces of his skin with them at Claude's direction. If Master gets the upper hand, neither of his minions' deaths will be pretty or painless—we'll suffer for this.

Claude wields the nanobots against Master brilliantly, and I use the distraction to attack. The bullets do nothing against the body armor he's wearing, but that doesn't stop Filip from trying. He and his men shoot at Master, regardless of the fact that I'm directly on the other side of him, ducking his punches. A bullet rips past me.

Somewhere above the insane noise of the infirmary, I hear Davian's voice as he directs his men in Filip's absence as he continues to launch bullets at Master, focused completely on killing the man and not on giving orders. If I can turn Master around so that his hood can't protect him, Filip might have a chance of killing him. If not, I have to end Master's life tonight, or we'll *all* be dead by morning.

"It was the king of Briarmar!" Claude shouts to Davian's men. He knows the odds are stacked against us, but perhaps one of them will survive to put an end to Briarmar's destruction. "He had planned to marry his daughter off to your prince and then kill the king and his son so his daughter would gain control. She'd never know and would listen to whatever he told her to do. It was a coup!"

Master ducks as I swing at him and I catch a peek of Filip's face as it all clicks for him.

"It wasn't Vila's fault!" I scream, making sure he knows she wasn't in on the plan. I truly believe her heart was too pure for her father to let her in on his secret.

Something crashes behind us just before Master's hand connects with my jaw. I hit the floor, the nanobots rushing to my defense as they form a mask around my face. If Master hits me now, he'll regret the pain that comes with it.

Claude rushes to me, picking me up off the floor. His fighting experience may be limited, but we both know Master better than anyone else in this room. My friend raises his fists, his dark features homing in on the man that controls our lives. Today, we gain our freedom in life or in death.

"I command you to stop!" Vila's voice fills the room.

"You can't command me to do anything, little girl," Master replies, his voice sounding eerily normal. "Not even your father can stop this. You're just lucky I haven't killed you yet. He didn't specify that I should spare you—he's your next of kin, so the line of succession would go to him anyway, and he'd have one less pesky problem to worry about."

"I speak on behalf of my father," she tries to say again, voice harsh.

"What did I just say, *girl*?" Master spits his words at her. "Leave or die with the rest of them."

My master's gun turns from me, training on the princess. Davian runs across the room, attempting to block the bullet. I reach forward just as the gun goes off, knocking it up. The bullet ricochets off the ceiling and slams back down into a table. The noise just encourages everyone else to attack.

Several men lay on the ground with bullets in them. A few are dead or close to it, but a handful only have minor injuries. I managed to distract Master enough that his shooting skills were thrown off during the fight and people are alive still because of it.

The rest of the men move to take him down as Davian runs toward Vila. He scoops her into his arms and forces her out of the room to protect her.

It feels empty in the room with them gone, but more guards join us, breaking into the room easily through the already-open door Master left behind.

Claude continues typing something into his wrist keyboard, and Master is frozen in place.

"I knew it would work!" Claude says out loud. I smile.

He always gets so worked up when his inventions work. He runs his fingers through his thick, black hair.

Unable to turn, Master stretches around, attempting to mow down anyone who approaches him. The gun pops as he moves, spraying bullets as men dive behind turned-over tables. I count.

One bullet left.

Filip counted too and instructs the men forward. They carefully move out from around the tables, slowly stepping toward the monster I call my master.

Davian bursts back into the room, but it's fallen deathly silent. Master doesn't even flinch. This is between the two of us now. He's already failed at his mission, and he doesn't have enough time to reach for more ammunition before the guards destroy him. His last act will be one of retribution.

The men move forward.

Master raises his weapon at me.

"One more step and she dies."

"Don't stop," I command the men. "Finish him."

Master doesn't waiver.

The men tackle him and Master pulls the trigger.

The nanobots race off my face toward my gushing wound. Davian's face falls in the distance as I reel backward. My eyes close before I hit the floor.

"That was stupid," Claude says, hovering over me. He's more emotional than usual. "You knew he would shoot you."

Pain courses through my body.

"An inch to the left and you'd be dead, Cindrill." Claude doesn't sound impressed by my bravado.

"But at least *he's* dead."

"Yes, they got him. It was miraculously hard, too, even frozen in place."

"You thought he'd go easily?" I wince as he moves the nanobots out of the hole in my chest. It feels like a million tiny insects are crawling inside of my injury.

"They'll be done soon." Claude softens. "*You'll* be done soon."

"Is everyone else okay?" I ask. My nose wrinkles as I cringe at the feeling again.

"Eight died, another six were injured. The prince is fine if that's what you're asking."

"Vila?"

"Confused, I hear." He dabs at my wound with a gauze pad. "She'll live."

"How does the king feel about her now?"

"From what Filip has told me, he's allowing her to stay. They will continue with the marriage, but the king already sent men to detain her father. In a perfect twist, he will use Briarmar's own plot against them and take control of their country."

My heart sinks...or maybe that's from the bots squirming an inch from that particular organ as they work their way to the top of the wound, crawling out of my skin as they close it up.

"Almost," Claude murmurs, leaning forward to examine me. "Just closing up the skin now."

He holds a container out against my shoulder and the nanobots that finished their work wheel themselves back inside. I close my eyes and breathe as the tiny pieces sew my skin together.

Glancing down, I realize all of the other bots have been taken from my body. The mark on my neck is exposed, as is the gash over my foot. Funny, Claude had time to fix my heart, but not my foot.

"You missed a spot." I motion toward my foot.

He tsks at me. "What precisely did you do to my shoe, madam?"

"You can blame Davian for that one. It's in my bag."

"Blaming me again, I see," Davian's dark voice breaks the discussion. "Seems everything is my fault these days."

His laugh holds no humor. Davian's eyes are darker than I remember. It's a terrifying picture.

"I hear you're getting married," I comment, trying to judge his reaction.

"I hear you're getting arrested for treason," he retorts, lips pursed.

"She saved you," Claude hisses at him.

"Careful, boy," Davian speaks down to my friend, even though he's clearly much older. "We haven't worked out all your crimes yet, but I suggest you let us focus on her."

Claude holds up the open container of nanobots, and they form a shape that appears to snap at the prince. My friend smirks as if the prince should be terrified, but Davian's lips just tug down, deepening his frown. "Don't tempt me."

"He didn't do anything, Davian," I say harshly, hoping Davian doesn't know Claude is the one who got the palace schematics for Master. "He's locked away in a basement creating wardrobe pieces and fixing nanobots. He's never hurt anyone. *I'm* the assassin."

Davian turns his cold eyes on me.

"Yes, I saw."

Walking closer, he glances at my foot and grimaces at the red scab he left. He turns to Claude. "Get out. I want a word with the assassin."

Claude straightens. "No."

"Go, Claude," I interject. "What's he going to do to me?"

He huffs, hovering for a moment before following my instructions. Claude leaves the open container of nanobots by my head, ready to take my commands.

"You lied this entire time," Davian says, gripping his hands behind his back.

"Did I have a choice?"

"How many people have you killed?"

"None personally." I try not to make eye contact, but his face is magnetic; I can't help but look. Everything softens, my face melting when I see him. Davian twitches slightly.

"You were going to kill me?"

"I was going to help," I admit. Davian steps closer.

"What changed?" He sounds as if everything in his world depends on my answer.

"I found out what was happening. I know the country has issues with you, Your Highness, but then I found out it was because you were protecting them from things they didn't need to know. When I learned it was Briarmar..."

"You decided not to do it," he finishes for me. "And you spared Vila...twice."

"She wasn't involved."

"I know," he says quickly, nodding. "She's the one who sent me in here."

"Why?" I question. The curtain shifts behind him as if someone walked by and created a breeze.

"Vila won't marry me. She says neither of us would be happy. She's agreed to form a treaty with me, and I've agreed to give her kingdom back to her as a sign of good faith as long as her father pays the price."

"You're going to kill him?" My eyes are wide. Davian looks shocked.

"No, who do you think I am, *you*? We don't *kill* people here. That's not how things are done," he chastises, taking a jab at me. "He will be held accountable for his crimes and will live in a dark cell just inside our border under our control and Vila's where she can easily visit him, but he can't do any more harm."

"So, Vila will rule, and you'll help her."

"I will."

"Why did she send you here, Davian. What good could that possibly do?"

I try to sit up but end up in a coughing fit. Surprisingly, it hurts less than I expect.

"You shouldn't do that right after being shot." His voice is quiet as he slips a hand behind my back to help guide me upright. I slip the strap of my shirt up over my shoulder, covering it. Claude must have taken me out of the rest of my outer layers to work on healing me with the nanobots. At least he left the half skirt wrapped around my pants—it's comforting to have it drape next to me.

I laugh coolly. "Wouldn't want me to die before my prison stint, huh?"

"I don't want to see you hurt, Cindrill." He lets go of the hard edges of his expression. "She sent me here because she thinks you and I belong together."

"And what do *you* think about that?" I'm still not sure where he stands.

Davian sighs, stepping backward with a slight limp. He walks around the foot of the raised cot, turning to move back again.

He holds the defaced shoe up from where he pulls it from the bag on the chair. The prince steps closer.

Davian slides the green, twisted shoe onto my injured foot.

"I knew I'd find you," he mutters, a smile tugging at his lips as he traces the skin next to what will likely end up as a scar. He turns to face me.

"I'm Davian," he says stepping toward me with an outstretched hand. "I'm the Prince of Davengreen, a fairly poor judge of when I should and shouldn't be running into buildings after pretty girls, and someone who tries to make things easier on others, even if it means getting pushed into a shuttle in the Epicenter that I'm not supposed to be on."

I take his hand, smirking as I think about the shuttle ride. His reintroduction is an offer to start over, one I'm happy to take advantage of without hesitation.

"I'm Cindrill—former assassin, excellent fighter, great judge of how far of a drop off a roof really is, and avid shuttle rider."

"Any chance you'd like to give me a few lessons on how to properly use the kingdom's shuttle system?" His eyes sparkle as he continues to hold my hand.

"You might be able to talk me into it," I reply, smiling up at him.

Maybe showing up at that palace to assassinate the royals *wasn't* the wrong choice after all. For now, though, I have to tell him how to catch the other assassins Master and I worked with.

Acknowledgements

I always knew there had to be a reason the prince didn't recognize Cinderella after he met her at the ball. I mean, he saw her face, so why wouldn't he? It took me a bit to figure out why he wouldn't be able to instantly know who she was the next time he saw her, but when I realized nanobots were involved, well…I was kind of thrilled. #techgeek

Cindrill gave me the opportunity to write another strong female lead, with all the girliness I love and all the power my readers crave. I hope you enjoyed this twisted take on her story.

Special thanks to Jess and Elle for all of your help—I know launching this one was a bit of a surprise, but I can't tell you how thankful I am that I can rely on your ladies every single time I need you (which is a lot…like, *a lot* a lot!)

If you loved Cindrill and Davian's story, I'd love to hear from you! Reach out and let's gush over them together! The best part about being an author is being able to talk about my characters with readers, so please reach out and share the fun with me!

Don't forget to check out my website for some special bonuses for Cindrill as well…I'm always rotating them out, so check back frequently for new gifts, freebies, and behind the scenes!

Stay inspired!
    -K.M. Robinson

WORLD PORTALS

Ready to learn exclusive facts about Cindrill and other K.M. Robinson Series?

World Portals are now available on
www.kmrobinsonbooks.com

Learn behind the scenes facts, watch videos, play games, check out our book filters, find out where to get bonus scenes, view fan art, and get access to other secrets we've hidden away inside the World Portals on the website.

The World Portals are constantly changing and information is being taken away and added all the time, so check back frequently for new content!

ABOUT THE AUTHOR

K.M. Robinson is a storyteller who creates new worlds both in her writing and in her fine arts conceptual photography. She is a marketing, branding and social media strategy educator who is recognized at first sight by her very long hair. She is a creative who focuses on photography, videography, couture dress making, and writing to express the stories she needs to tell. She almost always has a camera within reach. Visit her at her website: www.kmrobinsonbooks.com

CONNECT ON SOCIAL MEDIA

facebook.com/kmrobinsonbooks

instagram.com/kmrobinsonbooks

twitter.com/kmrobinsonbooks

Get free books and excerpts of other K.M. Robinson books at excerpt.kmrobinsonbooks.com

ALSO BY K.M. ROBINSON

The Jaded Duology

Book One: Jaded

Book Two: Risen

The Complete Series Boxset/Omnibus with exclusive epilogue

The Golden Trilogy

Book One: Golden

Forged: A Golden Novella

Book Two: Locked

Book Three: Edge

The Complete Series Boxset/Omnibus with exclusive bonus novella, Tempered

The Siren Wars Saga

Book One: The Siren Wars

Book Two: Darker Depths

Book Three: Beyond The Shores

Origins of the Siren Wars: Prequel Novella

Book Four: Forbidden Waters (coming soon)

The Legends Chronicles

Along Came A Spider: A Prequel Novelette

And They'll Come Home: A Prequel Novelette

The Archives of Jack Frost Series

The Revolution of Jack Frost

The Redemption of Jack Frost (coming soon)

Virtually Sleeping Beauty: A Novella Retelling

The Goose Girl and The Artificial: A Novella Retelling

The Sinking: A Novella Retelling

Cindrill (coming soon)

JADED: BOOK ONE OF THE JADED DUOLOGY

Her father failed in his mission to take control from the Commander, a defeat that has cost Jade her life. She will die as punishment. Now she belongs to the Commander's son—as his wife. Knowing his intent is to quietly kill her in revenge, Jade's every move is calculated to survive— until she learns her death ensures the safety of her father and her entire town.

Roan doesn't want to kill Jade, but once his family isolates her from her father and community, his only choice is to go through with the plan. Jade doesn't make it easy as she tries to sway him into falling for her. Each misstep makes him question his cause. Each moment makes every decision harder, but the Commander won't allow him to fail.

One chooses life. One chooses death. In the midst of the chaos, only one will succeed.

Now available!
Learn more about The Jaded Duology at
jadedinfo.kmrobinsonbooks.com

GOLDEN: BOOK ONE OF THE GOLDEN TRILOGY

Goldilocks was never naive. She was sent on a mission and Dov Baer is her new target.

When the girl with the golden hair betrays everyone, not even she has hope of surviving.

The stories say that Goldilocks was a naïve girl who wandered into a house one day. Those stories were wrong. She was never naïve. It was all a perfectly executed plan to get her into the Baers' group to destroy them.

Trained by her cousin, Lowell, and handler, Shadoe, Auluria's mission is to destroy the Baers by getting close to the youngest brother, Dov, his brother and sister-in-law and the leaders of the Baers' group.

When she realizes Dov isn't as evil as her cousin led her to believe, she must figure out how to play both sides or her deception will cause everyone in her world to burn.

If her allegiances are discovered, either side could destroy her...if the Society doesn't get her first.

Available now!
Learn more about The Golden Trilogy at
goldeninfo.kmrobinsonbooks.com

THE SIREN WARS: BOOK ONE OF THE SIREN WARS SAGA

War has hovered around the kingdom of Scylla for generations ever since the original sirens left the mer collection generations ago after nearly drowning the human prince. Over the years, select mermaids from the royal bloodline have been trained as spies to work for the reigning kings and queens, keeping the collection safe from sirens and humans.

Celena and her partner, Merrick, work covertly for the royals—not even her twin brother knows. When they discover the sirens have broken through the barriers the mer set up to keep the sirens out, Celena and her friends must race to the old kingdom of Metten to stop them from starting a war within their borders.

When she's dragged to the surface, Celena realizes that the war above the waters is as deadly as the one below the waves—and sacrificing herself may be the only way to protect her family.

The Siren Wars have only just begun.

Available now!
Learn more about The Siren Wars Saga at
sirenwarsinfo.kmrobinsonbooks.com

ALONG CAME A SPIDER: THE FIRST PREQUEL NOVELETTE TO THE LEGENDS CHRONICLES

Little Hacker Muffet
sat on her tuffet
destroying her cords and Way.
Along came a hacker named Spider,
who sat down beside her
and frightened his opponent away.

When Fet, one of the most skilled hackers in the Legends, discovers her best friend and leader of her group has been abducted and held for ransom, she must escape unnoticed and find Peep before it's too late.

When Spider, a new recruit training to join her hacker

ring, slips out with her and claims to have a plan to save her friend, Fet is forced to bring him along. As she discovers he's not who he claims to be, she faces grave danger and learns just how deadly a spider bite can be.

Now available!
Learn more about The Legends Chronicles at
acasinfo.kmrobinsonbooks.com

VIRTUALLY SLEEPING BEAUTY

She may be doing battle in the virtual world, but in the real world, they can't wake her up...

All Rora wants is to help people as class president, give her time to local charities, and quietly earn her way to the top level of the virtual reality system that the entire country uses without anyone noticing she's the second best player in the game.

All Royce wants to do is level up as a knight inside the gaming system, slay dragons, and eventually play his way to controlling the palace as he takes the crown away from the reigning queen.

When his Aunt Perry calls him, hysterically screaming that her goddaughter, Rora, has been inside for more than the four hours the game allows, Royce rushes over to help.

Entering the game, Royce soon discovers that Rora is trapped inside the system after an encounter with an evil magician who can change forms inside the game and control the virtual world. If he and his friend can't help her beat the game, she might not be able to wake up in the real world at all.

When virtual knights and princesses meet to slay dragons and defeat evil rulers, there's nothing stopping them from suffering real-world consequences too.

To wake her up, he must enter the game and help her beat it.

Now available!
Learn more about Virtually Sleeping Beauty at
vsbinfo.kmrobinsonbooks.com

THE REVOLUTION OF JACK FROST

No one inside the snow globe knows that Morozoko Industries is controlling their weather, testing them to form a stronger race that can survive the fall out from the bombs being dropped in the outside world—all they know is that they must survive the harsh Winter that lasts a month and use the few days of Spring, Summer, and Fall to gather enough supplies to survive.

When the seasons start shifting, Genesis and Jack know something is going on. As their team begins to find technology that they don't have access to inside their snow globe of a world, it begins to look more and more like one of their own is working against them.

Genesis soon discovers Morozoko Industries, but when a foreign enemy tries to destroy their weather program to make sure their destructive life-altering bombs succeed in destroying the outside world, only one person can shut down the machine that is spinning out of control and save the lives of everyone inside the bunker—Jack.

Now available!
Learn more about The Revolution of Jack Frost at
jackfrostinfo.kmrobinsonbooks.com

THE SINKING

The sea with wants to silence her, but not for the reason you think.

When a quirky older woman pawns a fancy seashell necklace at her mother's antique shop on the pier, Cara doesn't think much about the story the woman spins about the wearer turning into a mermaid.

On her way home, she accidentally drops the necklace into the ocean and is swept out to sea where she meets Quay--a merman who volunteers to take her to his mother, the sea queen, to help her get her legs back.

Cara soon learns that it's Quay's eighteen birthday--a day that has been a curse for his family--and is meant to be one for her too. Now she must fight to survive the sea with Quay at her side.

Fans of The Little Mermaid will love this twisted take on the beloved story.

Now available!
Learn more about The Sinking at
thesinkinginfo.kmrobinsonbooks.com

SUGARCOATED

Hansel and Gretel's witch...wasn't.

Annika's job is to create a cake to match the candy-colored rooftops, nightly firework shows, and daily parades ending in unexpected executions for the mad king's ball, but her true mission is to sneak a thirteen-year-old assassin into the palace using her gift of illusions.

Hansel's job is to protect his little sister, Gretel, once she assassinates King Levin and ends the destruction in Candestrachen, using his power over light to rescue the young girl from the chaos her influence over life and death will create.

When the entire forest reconstructs itself under Gretel's command while trying to save herself from a king's guard, Hansel and Annika must put their feelings aside and ensure their plan holds true—even if it means one of them has to sacrifice themselves to protect the mission.

Her illusions were meant to save her....but not everyone will survive the assassination attempt.

Learn more about Sugarcoated at
sugarcoatedinfo.kmrobinsonbooks.com